The Magdalene Secret

Jonathan Tallon

RICHARDSON JONES
PRESS

ISBN (large print hardback): 978-1-7392616-2-7

ISBN (paperback): 978-1-7392616-3-4

ISBN (ebook): 978-1-7392616-4-1

Chapter One

Professor Chelworth, dressed in browns from his brogues to his tweed jacket, peered over his tortoise-shell glasses, a frown clouding a usually jovial face.

'What do you mean, "it's gone"?'

I squirmed in my chair, trying to avoid his gaze. My eyes set upon an Edwardian portrait in dark oils behind him; the dignitary scowled down at me, framed by the ornate gilt.

'It's not there any more. I double checked.'

'You had better be bloody joking.'

His voice had taken on an icy quality, which was ironic, because the committee room seemed hotter and hotter. The oak-panelled walls were closing in. I could feel a trickle of sweat running down my neck.

'No joke. I'd just finished entering the basics into the database, and was about to take it over to imaging.'

'This is a disaster.'

I couldn't disagree. It was a disaster.

The professor pulled himself up from his chair, using the

mahogany meeting table as support, and sighed. He absent-mindedly started cleaning his glasses with his tie.

'How did you lose it? Papyri don't just get up and walk off by themselves for a stroll. They don't suddenly think, "I need a holiday" and wander out to find a taxi. So, again, what precisely do you mean by "it's gone"? Take me through it, in whatever detail you are capable of.'

This was not the professor with whom I was used to working. Less fun, more sarcastic. And definitely more furious. With good reason.

So I took him through my day.

It had started well.

That is an understatement.

The Monday had begun normally enough. A commute in on the 43 bus to Piccadilly Gardens, then a stroll across an overcast Manchester city centre to the John Rylands Library on Deansgate, grabbing a takeaway americano from Caffè Nero for a caffeine fix. A quick exchange of pleasantries with my colleague Maisy, then settling down to my work at my desk (the americano by now discarded; no drinks allowed near the work I was doing).

On my desk were a laptop, a ruler and a large, old, slightly stained cardboard box containing hundreds of scraps of papyri. My job for the next two years was to enter each one onto a database, providing a brief description and photograph, before ensuring safe storage for each papyrus in the library's specialised facilities. Once all were catalogued, we would begin to work out which would be worth translating and studying. So far forty-seven had been completed.

I opened up the box, the familiar hit of two-thousand-year-old dust hitting my nostrils, and picked up the top-most papyrus, a fragment about the size of a business card. The edges were frayed, and there were a couple of small holes. The writing on this papyrus was relatively clear; the darker brown, almost black, of the Greek letters contrasting with the oatmeal-coloured material.

All I had to do was give it a number (P. Ryl. VII 814), fill in the date (1st Century CE) and provenance (James Grove donation 2021, Hunt 1923) and add a brief physical description.

I wasn't meant to transcribe the Greek. That was due later in the process, after photographs, whenever we found time or another researcher could be funded to look at the collection. The John Rylands holds thousands of papyri, most catalogued but waiting for scholarly interest.

There are not many papyrologists world-wide. There are a lot of papyri.

I wasn't meant to transcribe the Greek. It wasn't in my job description.

But I did. It was a Monday morning, I was still trying to wake up, and cataloguing may have provided me with a two-year contract as a post-doc research associate, but was not the most gripping task intellectually.

So I transcribed the Greek. It was painstaking, slow work; the letters were unclear and there were a couple of gaps where holes had appeared in the papyrus.

...ΥΣΛΕΓΕΙΤΟΙΣΑΠΟΣΤ[...]ΣΗΜΑ
ΓΔΑΛΗΝΗΑΡΧΑΠΟΣΤΟΛΟΣΥΠ
ΑΚΟΥΕΤΕΑΥΤΗΩΣΗΜΑΓ[...]ΗΥ
ΠΑΚΟΥΕΙΜΟΥ...

My heart began to sprint like Usain Bolt. The translation was straightforward, but the implications...

'...us says to the apostles, 'Magdalene is the chief apostle. Obey her, as Magdalene obeys me.'

Stepping back from the table, I exhaled slowly, and gazed around the room, trying to imprint the moment into my memory. The functional laminate table. The cardboard box on one side. The oak-panelled walls. The aluminium laptop, cursor flashing in a box for database entry. The musty smell.

This was a moment to treasure.

I had discovered a fragment of a lost gospel, perhaps the Gospel of Mary Magdalene.

I would have been less ecstatic had I known that within the hour it would be gone.

Sitting down again, I spent another few minutes just staring at the fragment. The size of a business card, it was itself a card from the past. Two thousand years ago some early Christian community, probably in Egypt, had treasured their copy of the gospel.

And then it had ended up buried in sand (probably in some rubbish dump) until being dug up nearly 2,000 years later, before being sold in the first years of the twentieth century to British explorers who had packed it off in a cardboard box back to England. Where it had lain, untouched, unseen, for a further hundred years.

Until now.

The next step was to send out a quick email to my colleagues: Professor Chelworth, the director of the research project; and copying in Maisy Roberts, my fellow worker. That email used up my quota of exclamation marks for the year.

And after that, I needed to get a photograph of the papyrus in imaging.

Then came the knock on the door.

'Morning, Jake, no don't get up. Just giving a quick behind the scenes tour.'

And in bounced the professor, followed by a group of five adults.

'This is Doctor Andrews, a postdoc working on our latest project with Doctor Roberts,' the professor explained to the group, indicating first me and then Maisy, who had followed in at the end of the group.

It wasn't unusual to have groups come round the library. The John Rylands holds one of the greatest collections of written artefacts in the world; everything from Sumerian clay tablets through to trade union archives. You can find the first book printed in English by Caxton, or the first book to be printed using moveable type, and countless other rare and priceless collections.

The group mostly looked eager, despite it being a Monday morning. Three men and one woman were in dog collars. I guessed the outing had been arranged by some church organisation; that would make sense of Professor Chelworth showing them papyri, no doubt with a plan to finish with P52, a small triangular piece of papyrus reputed to be the oldest recorded fragment of the New Testament in the world.

Despite the professor's injunctions, I stood up, and introduced my work. Then followed about ten minutes of informal questions. One of the visitors, an American, the only one who wasn't a priest, then pointed at the papyrus fragment I had been working on.

'So what's that?' he asked.

'That... that is potentially interesting.' I decided to be cautious. 'The papyrus comes from a scroll rather than a codex...'

'What's a codex and how do you know?'

The interruption came from the woman. She was tall, wearing a black clerical shirt with a slip-in dog collar, black trousers, and an carrying a little leather-bound black note-book, making notes with a Bic. I tried not to react. Normally, we only allow pencils anywhere near the papyri.

'A codex is just jargon for a book. You don't see books before about the end of the first century. Before that, long documents were always scrolls, up to about 10 metres long'.

'A thirty-foot scroll?' The American. I wondered whether he had played American football at college. Something about the way he stood and his figure suggested alpha male sports in his background. And the gold Rolex on his left wrist screamed wealth.

'Yes. About thirty feet. We know this is from a scroll, because firstly there's nothing on the other side. Secondly, in the whole of this collection every papyrus appears to be from scrolls, all dating to the first century CE.'

Two of the clergy, the ones who appeared to be with the tall woman, winced when I said 'CE'. Although common in academic circles, the outside world still seemed to use and prefer 'AD'.

'So this papyrus,' I continued, 'is about two thousand years old from Egypt. And while it's early days, there might be some indications of it coming from a Christian community.'

Perhaps not that cautious. My brain was still buzzing with excitement.

Maisy looked up from her phone, where she had been surreptitiously checking messages. The professor frowned and peered over at the fragment. Neither of them had had a chance to read my email yet. Unless Maisy had just finished reading it...

The American stood stock still, his grey eyes focused on the fragment. Two of the clergy began to whisper to each other, taking on that look of faint surprise you show when you are trying to be polite and aren't really that interested. The tall woman frowned and made another note. The last cleric, a tall, striking man with dark hair, dressed entirely in black apart from the white dog collar, blinked and scribbled briefly on a small Moleskine branded notebook. In pencil, I noticed approvingly.

'Exciting stuff, as you can see...' said the professor, beginning to usher the small crowd towards the exit. 'Actually, Doctor Andrews, could you join us? We're going to the imaging office next, and I know you've had some experience with how helpful multispectral imaging has been.'

I joined the slow exodus from my office, the visitors now beginning to chat in quiet tones as the group moved onwards. Once we were all out, I locked up my office and joined the procession through the building, parrying the occasional question about my find, and trying not to look as excited as a puppy with a fresh squeaky toy.

It was more than an hour later that I returned to my office. I unlocked the door and prepared myself to check again the text of the papyrus, before mounting it ready for imaging.

My desk remained as I had left it; the laptop had entered sleep mode, but otherwise everything was untouched.

Except the papyrus was missing.

Chapter Two

'You've lost a bit of paper. That's what you're telling me?'

The sergeant looked a bit fed up. Her partner, a constable, seemed to be trying to hide a smirk.

'Technically it's not... ...yes, that's right.' I slumped back in the chair, and for the umpteenth time that day gazed at the committee room portraits, their Edwardian disapproval still glowering at me.

'I remember papyrus. We made it in primary school when we were doing the Egyptians,' chimed in her partner. 'We ripped up paper into strips, then soaked them in glue. Then we overlapped the strips and—'

'Thanks for that.' The sergeant was getting irritated. 'Why are we here, exactly?'

They were here because I had phoned the police, shortly before the professor had warned me not to. He had wandered off swearing under his breath when I had told him it was too late.

'Look, I know it seems trivial. But it could potentially be a crucial find.'

'Is it worth anything?'

'I don't know. We were still examining it. But potentially... maybe up to a million pounds?'

Now I had their attention.

The sergeant's eyes narrowed, and she straightened up in her chair. Then, leaning forward, hands clasped together on the mahogany table, she stared at me, head tilted to one side. Her partner took out a black pocket notebook. It seemed to be a day of notebooks. He also got out a black ballpoint pen. It didn't seem the moment to tell him that only pencils were meant to be used in this environment.

'A scrap of paper—that much?'

I wondered why the temperature seemed so high today. Usually, the inside of the John Rylands was cool even on the occasional Mancunian hot summer day. And this spring day was anything but that.

'Because it's old and comes from a batch all from the first century. Because it may be a fragment of a gospel. Because it may be the oldest Christian artefact we have.'

The constable sniffed in judgment when I said artefact. The sergeant continued to question me.

'Which gospel? Matthew, Mark, Luke or John?'

'None of them. The early Christian community produced loads of other gospels, mostly written a hundred or so years after Jesus. I think this was from the Gospel of Mary Magdalene. Possibly Philip.'

'Didn't hear about that from the nuns in school,' said the constable. He seemed to be treating the interview as a pleasant diversion from his usual duties.

The sergeant leaned back again. 'There's a Met unit that

deals with this, if they haven't been seconded again. A SOCO team will be along later to dust for prints.'

'Hieroglyphs.' The constable's statement came out of nowhere. 'I remember writing my name in hieroglyphs. Little pictures, like an owl. Is that's what's on this papyrus?'

'No. Greek.'

'Oh. Shame.' The constable was losing interest.

'Can I just recap? You found, you say'—I didn't like her emphasis—'a valuable papyrus. Only you saw it. You don't have any photograph of it. There's no other record of it. And it conveniently disappears from your office. Would you mind if we searched your bag and coat, Doctor Andrews?'

'Do I need a lawyer?'

'You haven't been charged yet. We're just looking for a little cooperation,' she said.

I slumped back.

'Go ahead. I'll fetch them now.'

'You won't mind if I accompany you back to your office.' This from the constable. It was more of a comment than a question.

Rising from the chair, I led the constable through the corridors to my office, trembling. Shivers started running up and down my spine. The temperature felt distinctly chillier.

Once inside the office, he pulled on a pair of latex gloves and picked up my battered, faded, navy Fjällräven rucksack. We left the office, and found an empty meeting room.

He began searching through my rucksack.

First out came a black clipboard with a small pile of white A4 paper, all blank. I used that for making notes in meetings or lectures. The constable carefully separated the pages out.

Next up were a collection of leads and connectors. Power

supply for my laptop; HDMI connector; VGA connector; USB-C to USB connector. The modern-day detritus of most people who present regularly and nomadically. He let these fall in a tangled pile on the desk.

Then came random stuff. A small box of ibuprofen (he checked inside the box). Some throat lozenges still in a blister pack, but having escaped the packaging some time ago. A face mask (disposable, light blue, not disposed of). A propelling pencil. An A4 battery. Another pencil, HB. A pack of tissues, unopened. A receipt for a Boost drink. A Caffè Nero loyalty card nearly completed (it had been near completion for a while; I now used their app).

The constable carefully placed each item separately onto the desk.

Last out was my A5 black notebook from WH Smiths, spiral bound with an elastic strap to keep it shut. As he held it, I wondered if I should upgrade to Moleskine notebooks. Somehow, it looked a little tatty and unprofessional in his hands. He undid the strap, held the book by its spine, and slowly waved it over the desk to allow any contents to fall out.

Gently, like an autumnal leaf floating from a tree, a scrap of papyrus drifted down.

For a moment, both of us stared at it.

The constable was the first to break the silence.

'Could this be the missing papyrus?'

Chapter Three

The constable continued to look at me, as he gently placed my notebook on the table next to the papyrus.

I tried to swallow, but the Sahara Desert seemed to have taken up residence in my throat.

'Could it have ended up in your notebook by... accident?'

I still couldn't speak. And my legs appeared to have had concrete poured into them. Second by second, my secure world was crumbling away.

The constable delved into a pocket and brought out a plastic evidence bag.

'We'll have to take this back and dust it for fingerpri–'

'No!'

My voice had come back.

'You can't cover that in your fingerprint dust. And you can't transport it in a plastic bag. You need acid-free, archival quality paper surrounding it. It's not just a hotel receipt.'

He looked at me, then sighed, as though dealing with stroppy researchers and bits of old paper was not what he had envisaged all those years ago when he had first chosen policing at a school career fair. Or perhaps it was the sigh of someone thinking to themselves that it was just another couple of years until retirement. Either way, it was not a happy sigh.

'Who do I see to sort this all out?'

'Me. Me or Maisy oversee all this. Or Professor Chelworth.'

'Well, it's not going to be you. Who's Maisy?'

'Doctor Maisy Roberts. She's my colleague on this project. She specialises in late antique Egyptian–'

'Where's Maisy?'

It took an uncomfortable ten minutes for others to track down Maisy, with me shuffling miserably from foot to foot in my room, overseen by the police officer standing upright, arms folded, scowling at me. The wait did not seem to be improving his mood.

Maisy entered the room, looked across at me with a slight frown, then smiled up at the constable.

'Hello, officer, I'm Doctor Maisy Roberts. How can I help you?'

'Officer Rushton,' he replied. 'Thank you for your time.'

So that was his name. I'd been so nervous when the police first arrived that the names of the officers had washed over me in a sea of anxiety.

The constable continued, 'how do I pack this papyrus safely? We need it to wrap up the investigation.' He pointed to the papyrus fragment.

'What are you planning on doing with it?' asked Maisy.

'Forensics will take a look. Fingerprints and so on.'

'No.' Maisy backed this up with a firm shake of her head. 'There's no way you're putting dust all over this. It's fragile, two thousand years old, and priceless. If it's part of the gospel of Mary Magdalene, there's only a handful of texts of this gospel worldwide, and this could be the earliest of them all. With respect, this needs to stay with experts.'

'Right, this is above my pay grade.' Another sigh. 'I'll check with my sergeant what we do next. At least we've found the papyrus.' He turned towards the door, grabbing the handle to open it. Meanwhile, Maisy was peering down at the table. In what was becoming a habit for this Monday, she frowned, shot me a puzzled look, and leaned over the table focusing on the fragment, before straightening up and addressing constable Rushton.

'This isn't the missing papyrus.'

Chapter Four

'What do you mean, this isn't the missing papyrus?' said the constable, turning back into the room.

Maisy ignored the constable, frowned (again), turned towards me, and said, 'That email. For real?'

I nodded. Maisy turned back to the papyrus, studying it again. Then, finally, she spoke to the police officer.

'It's different. For a start, the content is different. This looks like it's from a letter about household accounts. And, even without a ruler, it looks like a different size. A little bit bigger.'

I leaned forward for a better look. Rushton put out an arm. 'Don't touch it. You'll contaminate the evidence.'

Maisy shot him a withering look. 'As if. We're professionals here. No-one touches that without washing their hands first.'

Officer Rushton harrumphed, folded his arms together and glared at us.

Meanwhile, I was looking more carefully at the papyrus.

17

When Rushton had found it in my notebook, I had assumed it was the missing fragment. But Maisy was right. This was clearly different. Well, clearly different to anyone who worked closely with papyri.

'You're right. These are instructions about when to sow the fields. And there's more text than on my fragment,' I said. Maisy leant in closer, her interest piqued.

'Ooh, that's interesting. We've got a similar letter already in the Ryland collection. But that one's from a later century, second from memory.'

I was now even more confused. My find had gone missing, and another fragment had turned up in my bag.

'Did you pack this to study at home?'

Maisy was now interrogating me. Officer Rushton lifted an eyebrow, listening to our conversation carefully.

A shake of the head. 'I've literally no clue what's happening. I'd never do that.'

'Is this one you've catalogued?'

'Don't think so. I mean, it could be. Most of them I just enter the physical details in the database, then move to imaging. You know we're transcribing later. But it's not familiar.'

Rushton started telling his sergeant the situation over his radio. A couple of minutes later, she pushed open the door and marched in. As was now becoming traditional, she peered at the papyrus.

'How certain are you that this isn't the right one?' The question was directed at me.

'Certain.'

The sergeant repeated the question to Maisy.

'This is different. It's different content, and different size.'

The sergeant grimaced at the realisation that the case

wasn't going to be tied up quickly. She turned back to me, and straightened up.

'Okay, we'd like you to come to the station for an interview. Tomorrow at 10am. Oldham Road.'

'Wait, are you arresting me?'

I had never had any dealings with the police before. My knowledge of what happened in situations like this was limited to TV courtroom dramas, and most of the ones I had seen were American.

'No, this is a voluntary interview. You know the cliché: helping us with our enquiries.'

'Do I need a lawyer?'

At this point the sergeant sighed.

'You are entitled to have a solicitor attend with you. If you wish, the police will arrange for a solicitor to attend with you.'

'And if I say no?'

'Then we might decide to arrest you to make sure we can interview you properly.'

'I'd like a solicitor, please.'

This was not how I'd foreseen Monday turning out.

.

Chapter Five

I must have walked down through the John Rylands library from my office over a hundred times since I started my current job. But this time it seemed like a marathon. The walk of shame began by entering the reading room, a long, cathedral like gallery. From either side, marble statues of the greats of history glowered at me: Shakespeare and Milton; Newton and Dalton. And from either end the disapproving stone glare of John and Enriqueta Ryland.

The living, at least in my imagination, stared as coldly. The researcher in one of the alcoves, dressed up as a stereotype of an academic in tweed jacket with elbow patches. The two members of staff at the visitors' desk. I could feel my cheeks glowing scarlet. Surely they all knew why I was leaving the building early.

It was a relief that the lift was empty as I descended to the ground floor, before hurrying through the gift shop to escape, with shoulders hunched and eyes down to avoid catching anyone else's gaze.

Once outside I paused, staring up at the ash-coloured sky

and drawing in a lungful of cool air as considered what I should do next.

I didn't come up with anything.

I couldn't make sense of what had happened. How could the gospel papyrus have disappeared? And how did the other papyrus end up in my notebook?

My mind churning in rhythm with my stomach, I began to walk my route home. I started up Deansgate, staying on it a little longer than usual so that I could pop into Waterstones. I hoped the books might distract me.

Normally I tried to avoid this store; every time I went in I left considerably poorer financially if richer culturally. But today not even the displays of new books could entice me from my shame and confusion. I left through the exit on the other side of the shop, carrying on past St Ann's. A busker was massacring an Oasis song.

Soon I was on Market Street, the Arndale to my left, crowds swilling around. I paused outside Uniqlo, taking a moment to try to let my thoughts settle.

The crowd swirled around me, waves of shoppers and tourists. Then I noticed a woman walking purposefully towards me, eyes seemingly fixed on mine, approaching from the route I had just taken. Her long raincoat flapped around her as she strode forward, overtaking a woman pushing a buggy and a tall man dressed in black.

My stomach lurched again as it got hit by another dose of adrenalin. Was she really heading for me? Should I turn and run? But that would look ridiculous on a busy shopping street. And why was she approaching me?

Shame got the better of my panic, and I stayed still, waiting for her to approach.

'Hello, is it Doctor Andrews?'

This was delivered in a professional, no-nonsense way. No smile, no frown. I wondered what she wanted.

'I'm sorry, I don't think...'

'I'm Jemma Williamson, with the Manchester Evening Standard. Call me Jemma. I just missed you at the museum, and I've been trying to catch up with you. Would you have a couple of minutes to spare?'

This sentence she delivered with an enquiring smile.

I had more than a couple of minutes; I didn't know when I would next be able to work. But chatting with the press seemed like one way that I might actually be able to make things even worse for myself.

'I'm sorry, but I'm on my way home. Perhaps another time...'

I turned away from her and started walking again towards Piccadilly Gardens.

'That's okay, I'll walk with you.'

I had underestimated the determination of reporters.

'So, Doctor Andrews, I believe you work with papyri at the John Rylands?'

This felt safe to answer. I nodded as I walked along. Jemma kept pace, where necessary facing down oncoming shoppers in a low-stakes version of chicken. They always blinked first.

'And I believe that you discovered a fragment of a gospel?'

Word had travelled fast. I wondered how she had found out. Was it through eager museum staff, or good contacts with the police?

'We are still assessing a whole range of papyri from a recent donation by the Grove family.' I played it safe.

'Perhaps you could give me some background...?'

I sighed and paused my walking.

'Grenfell and Hunt were two British archaeologists who collected a whole range of papyri in the late nineteenth and early twentieth century, both through digging up ancient rubbish dumps and through buying up fragments from anyone who would sell to them. Some of these were copies of Christian writings, including parts of the New Testament. They sent their finds back to Britain. The John Rylands received some of them; others went to other museums, some to public schools, and some to private families.

'Hunt sent one collection that he'd bought in a street market to a college friend, James Grove. But before the collection arrived, Grove died in the tail-end of the 'flu epidemic after the first world war. Someone must have opened the box, seen some old bits of paper, closed it up again and put it in an attic.

'It was only rediscovered a couple of years ago, and the descendants of James Grove have now permanently loaned the collection to the John Rylands.'

I felt safe giving her all this information. It was all on the project website, meant for the public.

Jemma nodded encouragingly, making some notes in a spiral bound WH Smith reporter's notebook. It was comforting to know both that other people also used cheap notebooks, and that reporters actually did use reporter's notebooks.

'But now a major find from the collection has gone missing. Could you give me some background on this as well?'

Back to dangerous territory.

'I'm sorry, in the circumstances I'd prefer you speak to the police rather than me.'

'So, the police are involved... thank you for confirming that the museum is taking this seriously.'

I silently swore to myself. I should have just no commented.

'Doctor Andrews, what is it like to hold the earliest Christian fragment? Could you describe your emotions for our readers?'

The memory of the morning's excitement briefly washed over me again, to be followed by a flood of doubt and anxiety.

'I think you'd be better off talking to Professor Richard Chelworth. He's the guy heading up the project.'

'Oh, I will. But I thought you might appreciate giving your side of the story.'

What did she mean by that?

'What do you mean by that?'

'Well, this is going to be a major story. It's got a mysterious case of papyri with secret gospels that could alter the history of Christianity. And someone's nicked them. And you were the last person to see these gospels. You're at the centre of the story. And not necessarily in a good way.'

I thought the day couldn't get worse, but hearing this made me realise I was wrong.

'I shouldn't be talking to anybody.' With this, I started walking again. Jemma placed her notebook into a bag slung across her shoulder, and started up after me again.

'Okay, I can see that now isn't the right time for you. But you may want to change your mind. I'm trying to do you a favour, get ahead of the story. When you realise I'm on your side, I'll be ready to listen.' And she produced a business card. I accepted it, hoping that this would end the interrogation, and shoved the card into a trouser pocket.

We were nearly at the bus terminus now. She stopped, and smiled again at me.

'Goodbye Doctor Andrews. I look forward to hearing from you. And... good luck.'

I grimaced in return, before joining the queue to board the number 43 bus. I turned back to see Jemma stride away, her long coat still flapping around her. I shook my head, and climbed onto the bus, ahead of three giggling teenagers, an older woman carrying six shopping bags, a tall man dressed all in black reading a copy of the free Metro, and a young man having a loud argument over his phone.

As I sat down at the front upstairs, a thought began to niggle at me. Hadn't I seen the man dressed in black before?

Chapter Six

There's nothing like a good dose of adrenalin still flowing through your body to fuel paranoia. Maybe I was starting to put two and two together and making twenty-two.

I took a deep breath, slowly exhaled, and tried to take stock. I was certain I had seen a man in black behind me on Market Street, and now again on the bus. Could it be someone from the morning visit to the John Rylands? One of the clergy? I wished I had checked whether the man had been wearing a dog collar.

The bus began to weave its way through the city centre before turning onto Oxford Road to head south. I looked around. The three teenagers had also moved to the upper deck, and had ensconced themselves on the back seat. One in the middle was holding up a phone, and all three were watching it, with periodic outbreaks of laughter. From down-stairs, the sound of the young man raging into his phone drifted upwards. But on my deck, there was no sign of the man in black. He hadn't followed me upstairs.

My heart was still pounding away. Another deep breath. More thinking. Even if the man had been one of the John Rylands visitors this morning, was that significant?

If it was him, well, thousands of people come in and out of south Manchester on the buses up and down Oxford Road every day. Perhaps every hour. The local legend held that it was the busiest bus route in Europe. If the man had been one of the visiting ministers, chances were that it was coincidence.

I took another deep breath, another slow exhale. The rational side of my brain was clear. There was no reason for anyone to be following me; I had no real idea if the man in black was from the visit this morning; if he was, it would be one of those random connections, meaning nothing.

Another loud peal of laughter came from the teenagers.

Despite my efforts to calm myself, the less rational side of my brain was not happy. And, in a contest between pure reason and adrenalin-fuelled anxiety, anxiety wins out every time.

The bus was by now making its way past the Royal Northern School of Music and Manchester Aquatic Centre, making good progress with only other buses and cyclists allowed on this stretch of Oxford Road. I pressed the stop button on the yellow pole behind me, and made my way down the stairs, trying not to look around.

As the bus pulled to a halt, I moved forward to the doors. As soon as they opened, I strode out, thanking the driver, then turning right to continue down Oxford Road. After about fifty paces I paused and turned as if wanting to cross the road. This gave me the chance to glance back to see who else had disembarked.

A tall man was ambling in my direction from the bus

stop, clutching a copy of the Metro. As he was approaching face on, I was able to see a white dog collar contrasting with his black clothes. He was a minister. And one I recognised. He was one of the four ministers visiting the John Rylands earlier on.

The rational part of my brain gave up even trying at this point.

I was being followed. And I had no idea why.

Chapter Seven

If anxiety trumps reason, then not wanting to make a scene trumps anxiety. The primal part of my brain was screaming 'run', but I was worried that I would look ridiculous. What did I have to be frightened of? The man wasn't threatening me, or even moving particularly fast towards me. If anything, he was ambling, newspaper still in hand.

I turned away, and continued to head south down Oxford Road, keeping up a good walking pace, hoping to put a little more distance between myself and my pursuer.

I kept being tempted to turn around and check, so I made myself count to 500 steps before pausing again, and took a glance back up the pavement.

He had gone. There were a few students gathered in small groups, carrying bags and chatting, and a couple of women pushing buggies, also chatting, but no-one in black. I scanned both sides of the road, and waited for a few seconds, but he had disappeared. It seemed I was no longer being followed.

Puzzling over this, I continued walking down Oxford Road, until I reached another bus stop. Within a couple of minutes, another 43 pulled up. I flashed my pass, got on, and found a downstairs seat. My heart was still racing (not helped by the fast-paced walking), but it no longer felt as though it was pounding loudly.

As the bus continued rattling its way through Rusholme's collection of Indian and North African restaurants and cafés, my anxieties subsided further. I had allowed myself to be spooked by all the events of the day.

A glance out of the window gave a further focus to aid relaxation. By now the bus was rolling past Platt fields, with a line of trees that had all recently come into glorious pink blossom. A brief gust shook the trees, as if they needed to shiver, and a snow cloud of petals drifted to the ground.

And then it was my stop. Just past Owens Park, the large student accommodation buildings, and just before the cross-roads where the nightclub/bar changed hands every couple of years. I crossed over the road and made my way down one of the terraced streets leading off the main road.

At one time, these had been solid working-class homes, close to the old home of Manchester City. But in more recent years City had moved out, and students and others had moved in. I shared an end of terrace house with Pete, who had arrived in Manchester as an undergraduate and never escaped its pull. Nowadays he seemed to eke out a living doing occasional DJ gigging interspersed with some zero hours jobs.

But this week I would be spared the stink of weed seeping out of his bedroom and leaving its pungent aroma infecting the whole house. He was away visiting his parents in Aberystwyth.

I had my hand in my pocket for the door key when my phone beeped. An incoming message. I glanced at the screen: it was from Maisy.

r u OK? Call if you need to.

I smiled. It was good to have at least one person on your side.

Thanks – appreciated :)

Then I noticed I had missed an earlier text, from Pete.

Don't forget to feed Mr B!!!

I sighed, slipped my phone back in my pocket and got out the key.

Which wasn't needed.

Someone had already forced open the door.

Chapter Eight

Seeing the door lock with wooden splinters everywhere didn't help calm my nerves after an already eventful day.

I gently pushed open the door, staying on the threshold.

'Hello? Anybody there?' I'd rather give any intruders the chance to escape than risk a confrontation.

The house remained silent. I crept into the hallway and flicked the light on.

'Hello?'

Still no reply.

I pushed open the door to the right, leading to the front room. Pete had converted this into a home cinema set up. There was a large flat screen TV trailing a spaghetti bundle of wires, sound bars, small wireless speakers everywhere, a PlayStation and controls, and one large, slightly grubby, tan coloured sofa. On the magnolia walls were a couple of Tarantino movie posters: Pulp Fiction and Reservoir Dogs. The floor was wooden floorboards covered in the centre with a cream rug that had seen many better days.

Everything was still in place, roughly. The cream rug had been moved, and sofa cushions were on the floor. One side of each of the posters had been ripped from the wall, leaving a little oily mark where they had been attached. But the TV was still there. The speakers were intact. The PlayStation hadn't been taken.

Either the intruders were highly incompetent burglars, or something else was going on.

I moved on to the second room, again on the right as I went further along the hallway.

This was my study. Over my years acquiring the various degrees necessary for my job (undergraduate, masters, PhD) I had developed a book addiction; one shared by many in academia. The wall to the left as you entered was entirely bookshelves. I organised by subject area, so one section was primary sources in original languages, another was translations of texts, another on late antique religion, and so forth. The books jumped in size and style, giving a slightly chaotic visual appearance, but it all made sense in my mind.

An ex-girlfriend had once rearranged all my books by size and colour while I was away at a conference. When I arrived back, she almost hopped with excitement as she explained how much better the room looked.

It wasn't the reason why we split up, but it certainly didn't help.

Straight ahead as you entered, facing a bay window, was my desk. This was a functional pine affair with round metal legs, courtesy of IKEA. An LED angle lamp perched on one side, and a pile of random bits of A4 paper, full of scribbled notes that had made sense at one point in time, covered the rest. A blue desk-chair on wheels completed my working space.

No-one had stolen any of my books. This wasn't really a surprise, but it was a relief. Academic books are expensive. It is quite usual for copies to be eighty pounds upwards. Some days I dreamed of winning the lottery just so I could afford books published by Brill (I would have a better chance if I actually entered).

But some books had been moved. A few had been taken out, as if checking that nothing was behind them. The papers on the desk had been lifted and dumped down again, with one or two having drifted to the floor. No real damage, and nothing missing.

I came back out of my study and debated whether to check the kitchen or upstairs first. Upstairs won the mental toss of a coin. Slowly, and noisily (I really didn't want to surprise any intruders), I climbed the stairs.

The first-floor layout mostly mirrored that of downstairs. Pete's bedroom sat above the front room; my bedroom was above my study and the bathroom and loo were above the kitchen area.

First, Pete's room. I cautiously pulled down the door lever and nudged it open.

I had managed to disperse the smell of weed from the rest of the house, but it still lingered here. The aroma caught in my throat, and I coughed.

The room was a mess. T-shirts and jeans lay scattered on the floor and un-made bed. Every drawer in the chest had been pulled out. Pillows that should have been on the bed had made their way to the floor. One curtain had been pulled back; another still provided privacy and shade.

Truth be told, I was finding it difficult to tell if the room had been touched. Pete was messy at the best of times. I backed out and opened the door to my room.

A similar scene greeted me. Clothes covered the floor, torn from drawers that were pulled out and now mostly empty. The duvet had been dragged back and dropped.

I am by no means the tidiest person in the world, but I am not particularly messy either.

Someone had been going through my possessions.

I backed out and turned towards the bathroom. Here, the door of the wall-cabinet was ajar.

And then, from downstairs, a thud. A few seconds, and another thud. And another. The noise seemed to vibrate through the walls.

I sighed. That was probably Mr B.

I returned downstairs and entered the kitchen area. This consisted of an eating area (dining room would be upgrading its status) leading to a narrower galley style kitchen with dark grey units. In the main space, a battered pine wooden table still had my dirty dishes and mug from a quickly grabbed breakfast. Four pine chairs surrounded it.

And in the corner, in a cage with a red plastic base and white wiring, came another thud.

Mr B was a bad-tempered rabbit that Pete had bought on a whim. The bunny's full name was Mister Binkipops, that had seemed amusing for the first couple of days after his arrival when we had assumed that the rabbit was a cute bundle of fluff, rather than a grey fur ball with claws and teeth, and the manners of an aggressive sleep-deprived toddler.

Mr B was currently demonstrating his dissatisfaction with life by stamping his left hind leg repeatedly.

Rabbits are generally quiet pets, in that they don't bark or meow or howl at the moon. But they do stamp when they're angry or frightened. Mr B often seemed to be angry.

I looked at Mr B. He stopped thumping and looked at me, nose twitching away. Then, staring straight into my eyes, he slowly and deliberately lifted up his left hind leg and brought it down with a solid bang.

Further investigation would have to wait. I took an apple from the fruit bowl (I was the only one who either remembered to restock it, or, as far as I could tell, to eat the fruit; Pete never touched it), cut off a couple of slices, opened up a hatch in the white wires and dropped the slices in the cage. Mr B sniffed around, picked one up, and scurried into a covered area quickly in case anyone tried to take the slice away. At least the thumping stopped.

That sorted, I took another look at the room, and took a bite from the remains of the apple. Some of the kitchen cupboard doors were open, and so was one of the drawers.

And there was a post-it note on the kettle.

I don't put post-it notes on kettles, and Pete never bothered leaving notes of any kind.

Scrawled in biro on the bright yellow background was a direct message: 'WHERE IS IT?'.

Chapter Nine

I stared at the yellow post-it note, questions swirling through my mind. Who was so desperate to get the papyrus, and why did they think I had it? And how did they know where I lived?

I wasn't sure about calling the police at first, but I decided I had better report it. If nothing else, it might keep the landlord off my back about the broken lock if I had a crime number.

First, I returned to my study, found an envelope in my stash of stationery, and took it back to the kitchen. Gingerly using some metal tongs, I transferred the note to the envelope, and switched on the kettle. I needed a coffee.

While the kettle started to chunter away, I called the police line. They didn't sound terribly interested when they found out that nothing had been stolen, and couldn't promise that it warranted anything like dusting for fingerprints; apparently the team was already overstretched. But at least I'd eventually get a crime number.

I poured a few teaspoons of grounds into my cafetiere

mug, added the boiling water, and realised I was hungry as well as thirsty. No wonder. I had missed lunch at the John Rylands while waiting around for the police to turn up and conduct their interviews. I investigated the fridge while waiting for the coffee to brew. There were a couple of eggs and a small hard lump of cheddar that could be fashioned into a meal.

I pushed down the plunger on the cafetière, and wondered if the satisfying feeling from doing this was the true reason why I liked real coffee. Then I got out a small frying plan, cut off a knob of butter into the centre, whipped up the eggs in a small bowl, and found the cheese grater. The comforting smell of melted butter soon filled the air.

Ten minutes later I was sitting at the table, finishing off my coffee and eating the last morsels of a cheese omelette. It wouldn't win any culinary awards, but at least I was no longer starving.

The events of the day were still hanging over me like a dark cloud, so I decided to face them head on. I moved to my study, found a fresh sheet of A4 paper and a stubby pencil, and made a list of all the people who could have known about the papyrus.

It wasn't that long. Just my colleagues, and the party of visitors. And the two police officers. Unless someone had told another member of staff at the museum?

But someone had also leaked the information to the newspaper. The circle of people who might have known was wider than I had initially thought.

But who had time to find my house and break in before I got home? And how did they think I had managed to hide it at home if I was still at work when they broke in?

None of it made any sense.

I scrumpled up the paper into an irregular ball and dumped it in the waste-paper basket.

Time to try to relax. I moved to the front room, returned the cushions to the sofa, turned on the TV, and settled down to a repeat of The Big Bang Theory. I stayed there, slumped, letting the programme wash over me, and feeling my eyelids starting to droop.

I woke with a start in darkness to a loud noise. The television was still burbling away. A check on my watch showed it was now 3am.

The noise was Mr B again. He needed some fresh hay and water. I sorted him out, and traipsed to bed, falling onto it still dressed, and was asleep within seconds, images of papyrus fragments spinning through my thoughts.

Chapter Ten

I woke the next morning to the insistent tones of my phone. Reaching out an arm, I grabbed it, and looked to turn off the alarm.

It wasn't the alarm. Maisy had texted me. I checked the time: 6:45am. This was unusual. I knew Maisy was an early riser, but she also knew I wasn't.

check MES u r viral!!!

In my drowsy state, this didn't make much sense. I yawned, stretched, and wiped some sleep from my eye. Sitting up in the bed, I looked at her text again.

And realised that *MES* stood for the Manchester Evening Standard. I switched over to the browser and typed it into Google. And there, as the first headline, was the story.

Found and Lost: Secret Gospel discovered and stolen from Manchester Museum!

I quickly scanned the article. I appeared in the second paragraph, as a researcher who was the last person to be with the fragment. In the next paragraph, we were told that a thirty-two-year-old man was to have a voluntary interview with the police. It wouldn't take Sherlock to put two and two together.

To be fair to Jemma Williamson, who had the by-line, the information throughout was fairly accurate. It just wasn't a good start to the day.

Pulling a dressing gown on, I wandered downstairs, bunged a couple of slices of thick, white bread in the toaster, and grabbed some orange juice from the fridge. While waiting for the toast, I started to plan out the day. Rather than going straight to the police station, I decided to go into work first thing, to show my face.

And perhaps return some normality to my life.

The slices jumped up, now with an extra tan, and I took some Flora margarine from the fridge and smeared it over the toast. Mr B looked up, twitched his nose, and shifted his left ear at the scraping noise. Sighing, I walked over to the bag of hay next to the hutch, grabbed a big handful, and shoved it in the little wire trough. Next up was refilling the water bowl. Then some rabbit nuggets. Then, after some rooting round the fridge, a handful of spinach. I took more care over making sure the rabbit had a healthy diet than my own. And he wasn't even my bunny.

I gave his silky soft fur a stroke, and I was rewarded with him turning his back on me. While Mr B furiously guzzled down the nuggets, I returned to my own breakfast. But the toast was dry in my throat, as anxiety kept unsettling my stomach.

I threw the second slice in the bin, finished up the orange juice, and returned upstairs.

A shower and shave later, and now fully dressed, I went to leave the house. It felt strange leaving without my rucksack, but the police still had it.

I went to lock the door, and then remembered that it had been forced. I made a mental note to call the landlord and hoped that no-one else would break in while I was away.

As I turned from the front door, my neighbour emerged, muscles rippling in a ragged t-shirt and boxers.

'Jake, glad to catch you.'

'Hi. What is it, Mo?'

'Couple of guys were hanging around your place yesterday. Just wanted to check you're okay.'

I paused for a second while I took in the information.

'Thanks. They broke in, but nothing appears to be missing. Maybe you disturbed them somehow?'

'Dunno. I just came out to buy some cigs, and when they clocked me, they wandered off.'

'I might need some info for a crime report.'

'Heavies. Both white, about my height, solid muscle. About 3pm, because I'd got back from my shift. But I don't want to get involved with anything official.'

'Listen, thanks mate. It's appreciated.'

Mo wandered back inside. I wasn't surprised the two men had left when Mo had appeared. He was well over 6 foot and built like a heavy-weight boxer. Not someone to mess with if you didn't have to. He was currently working at a local supermarket while trying to start a career as a performance poet. Pete and I had seen him at a pub open night a few weeks ago, and been impressed.

Mulling over the new information, I walked up the street to the main road. I dropped into the newsagent (more like an off-licence that also sold other stuff) and bought a paper copy of the Manchester Evening Standard. If I was going to be in the paper, I might at least keep a copy as a souvenir of this time.

The queue for the buses had twenty people lined up, mostly students. Two buses arrived within the next minute, and I hopped on the second one, picked up the free newspaper from the pile at the front of the bus, and climbed to the top deck, finding a space right at the front. Settling down, I checked to see if I was also in this paper. There was no mention of the story. I hoped it was a sign that press interest would blow over almost instantly. The quick crossword took up the rest of the journey time as the bus worked its way up Oxford Road and then threaded its way to Piccadilly Gardens.

The walk from there to the John Rylands gave me an opportunity to relax some more. Once I was nearly there, outside Caffè Nero, I thought about getting an espresso first, when a deep, masculine voice with an Italian accent hailed me.

'Doctor Andrews, could I have a word?'

The speaker was the tall cleric dressed in black who had followed me yesterday.

Chapter Eleven

I glanced around warily, but the mysterious cleric seemed to be alone. Office and shop workers trickled past, but no-one that remotely fitted the description of a heavy.

'How did you know I'd be here?'

'What?' He sounded surprised to be asked.

'And I'm sorry, but I don't think I know your name.'

'Father Augusto Zappacosta. And I didn't.'

'Didn't what?'

'Know you'd be here. I came to get a coffee, and recognised you from yesterday.'

I didn't know whether to believe him, but he didn't appear immediately dangerous.

'How can I help?'

'Perhaps over a coffee? Let me buy you one, yes?'

He confidently strode into the café, and after a small pause, I trailed after him. At least it looked like I would get a free cup out of it.

A couple of minutes later, we were sat in the twilight

lighting of the café at a small, square table, sipping black espressos.

'I wanted to know a bit more about the papyrus find. The newspaper suggested it was a lost gospel. Is that so?'

People clearly did read the local newspaper. At least, both Maisy and Father Augusto did.

'I'm not sure how much I should say. If you've read the paper, you'll know that police are involved. I don't want to tread on their toes.' I wondered as I said it if later in the morning the police would be treading on my metaphorical toes.

'And can I ask why you're interested?' I continued.

'I'm the Deputy Secretary of the Dicastery on Scriptural Literacy and Education.'

I looked at him blankly.

'I'm with the Vatican, looking at how we help people learn about the Bible,' he said.

That would explain why he had been part of the small party yesterday being given access behind the scenes to the work Maisy and I were doing at the John Rylands.

He continued, 'Well, if you cannot talk about that fragment, maybe I could interrogate you about other fragments, yes?'

I warily agreed, and we spent the next half an hour with him asking about some of the other finds that the John Rylands held, and what their significance was. Father Augusto listened intently to the answers, occasionally making notes in his Moleskine notebook.

Finally, I looked at my watch, and announced that I had to go. As we were standing up, he locked eyes with mine, and said, 'We are extremely interested in that lost fragment. Extremely. Please do contact me if there is any news.'

And with that he handed over a business card, shook my hand, pronounced how pleased he was to meet me, then strode off, heading north up Deansgate. I glanced at the card, and shoved it into a pocket. Taking a deep breath, I headed over the road towards the John Rylands building.

As I entered the glass atrium, my self-consciousness began to rise. Was that a knowing glance from the woman operating the shop till? And was that a frown on Pete the security guard's face as he greeted me? Pete moved towards me.

'Jake, do you mind just waiting here rather than going up? Professor Chelworth asked to catch up with you here when you arrived.'

I was right. The security guard had been frowning. I took a seat, wondering what exactly was going on. But almost as soon as I sat down, Professor Chelworth appeared. It seemed to be a day for frowns; he was wearing one on his face too. I stood up as he greeted me.

'Jake, good to see you. Hope you're bearing up.' He seemed to be treating me as though I were in mourning. 'I've got something to tell you. With all that's going on, we, that is the board, decided that it might be best for you to take a little time away from the museum for a few days.'

'That's kind, but I think I might be better just getting my head down and carrying on with my work,' I replied.

'This isn't really a choice.'

I fell silent. Professor Chelworth stood there, not saying any more. Eventually I filled the vacuum.

'I'm being suspended.' I made a statement, rather than presenting it as a question.

'I'm afraid, under the circumstances...'

His voice trailed off, and he briefly shifted his weight

from one foot to the other. Then he began to speak again, slightly faster than usual.

'Also, the board is meeting this Friday to review your contract. They are going to consider whether it might be better for everyone for us to part ways.'

I took a large breath.

'But I haven't done anything – why is the board acting like this?'

'We have a reputation to consider. And, with due respect, the papyrus did go missing from your office, and another one was found in your bag, in clear contravention of our policies about papyrus handling.'

I sat back down again, my mind beginning to race. In three days, I was going to be an unemployed papyrologist. I imagined that there would be limited opportunities for this specialism at the local Job Centre. As though reading my mind, the professor spoke up again.

'I mean, look on the bright side, you might find you earn much more outside academia. Finance seems to pay well. And it's not like they pay us much, do they?' he said, as I remained silent.

Professor Chelworth adjusted his tie slightly, pushed his glasses firmly up against his nose, and then looked down at the floor for a few seconds.

'Well, I suppose it's a bit of a shock. I'll... I'll let you take it all in. It's a lot to process, but I'm sure you'll see that we... that they had no choice.' All of this was said without looking up at me. Then, he turned around, and shoulders slightly slumping, walked slowly away.

I stayed sitting there for a few minutes, thinking bitterly about how different life had seemed only twenty-four hours previously. Now, I was even shut out of my own office.

Finally, I stood up, and wandered outside, past Pete who gave me an apologetic shrug.

A faint sun was battling valiantly to break through the Manchester clouds, and mostly failing. A gentle breeze blew a discarded crisp packet around my feet, where it danced chaotically for a few seconds before moving on. I checked the time. It was still only 8:30am. Still an hour and a half until the police interview, and it was only a twenty-minute walk away. I decided to head up Deansgate to the cathedral, hoping to find a quiet space to be able to gather my thoughts.

As I entered the cathedral, the constant background noise of cars and trams fell away. Seats had been laid out for a service later that day, so I sat down on a wooden chair, and looked up at the renovated organ.

Out of the corner of my eye I noticed someone approaching. They sat down on the chair on my right. I shifted slightly to my left. Then, in a soft, American drawl, 'Doctor Andrews, we need to talk.'

Chapter Twelve

I turned to look at the speaker. I was surprised the chair was sustaining his bulky frame, so heavy was his presence. A charcoal grey suit tried valiantly to cover his muscular torso and arms. His sandy coloured hair was cropped short, reminding me of marines in films I had seen. He had a superhero's jaw, and pale grey eyes.

'I'm Brad Ryan. I saw you yesterday at the Library.'

'I remember. You were part of the group touring round.'

He shifted in his seat, and turned more towards me.

'Let me get straight to the point. I represent an individual with a particular interest in Biblical artefacts. I have been authorised to negotiate with you over the papyrus fragment.'

I looked away briefly, focusing on the abstract oranges and reds of one of the stained-glass windows. Everyone seemed to think that I had the missing gospel piece.

'Who is this "individual"?'

'A person of considerable means. They intend to create a collection to rival the Museum of the Bible, only this will remain private rather than open to the public. And the individual does not want their identity to become public.'

'And you don't care whether you get stuff for your collection legally or not?'

'My client has nothing but respect for the law. We would be happy, though, to pay a consultancy fee that might lead to a valuable acquisition.'

I was intrigued. I had heard, of course, about the often murky world of buying and selling papyri. In my field, people gave conference papers about the importance of provenance. In some high-profile cases, museums had been forced to return items back to the countries from which they had been illegally taken. Combined with this was a healthy trade in forgeries, as entrepreneurial criminals sought to create supply to keep up with the demand. But I had never been directly involved before. I wondered how much I would be worth if I had taken the fragment.

'How much would such a consultancy fee be?'

'Assuming that the piece turned out to be genuine, then fees can be as high as one hundred thousand dollars.'

I nearly gasped, but managed to control my reaction. One hundred thousand was just his opening offer. Thoughts of paying off student debt, deposits for a house, a decent holiday, all flitted through my head. Not that it mattered in practice, of course. And anyway, I wouldn't, even if I could. At least, I told myself I wouldn't, and pushed down a small, nagging doubt that I would be easily tempted.

'I would love to be able to help your client', I began, untruthfully (I hoped it was untruthfully), 'but I'm afraid that you're mistaken. I'm not in a position to be able to offer "consultancy" to your client.'

He laughed. Somehow, it did not come across as a friendly laugh.

'But you're the expert here. You have...', he paused for a second, searching for the right word, 'unique knowledge to be able to help my client.'

'I'm glad you think I have this unique knowledge. I don't have anything that's unique, so I'm not able to help your client.'

He tilted his head to the left slightly, and looked directly at me, unblinking. After an uncomfortable pause, he looked up to the cathedral ceiling, sighed, and pushed his right hand into his left internal breast pocket, withdrawing a business card. He offered the card to me.

'If you should find yourself in a position to offer consultancy, call me. My client is generous, but impatient. And is used to getting what they want.'

I accepted the card, and shoved it into a pocket, where it joined the ones I had already collected. It seemed to be the day for business cards. I was more used to exchanging phone contacts.

He stood up, and thrust out his right hand. I weakly proffered mine, and he grasped it firmly and shook it up and down three times.

'Goodbye Doctor Andrews. Please be in touch. We won't wait forever.'

And, leaving the threat hanging in the air, he turned and walked away to the exit.

I had gone to the cathedral hoping for a little oasis of calm after the last twenty-four hours, but now the gothic architecture took on more sinister overtones, as I tried to process what was going on. I stood up, and headed out to the daylight.

I glanced at my phone to check the time, and started heading east towards the police station. I wondered if I would cap a miserable couple of days by ending up in a cell.

Chapter Thirteen

The woman sitting at the stained Formica table opposite me did not inspire confidence. She had already dropped her pile of papers on the floor or desk three times, apologising profusely on each occasion. This was Ms. Anita Foster, my appointed solicitor for the interview. She perused some paperwork.

'Mister, uh, oh no, it's doctor, isn't it? Yes, doctor. Doctor. Doctor Jake Andrews. Is that a medical doctor? Oh no, silly me, of course it's not. Not with your case. Doctor Andrews. A pathologist. Oh, are you a medical doctor?'

I briefly interrupted the stream of expressed thought: 'No, not a medical doctor. And it is papyrologist, not pathologist'.

'As long as I get the gist of it,' she replied, and then laughed at her own joke.

I didn't laugh.

'Right, take me through what happened in your own words.'

I recounted the events of the previous morning. Anita made notes on a straw-yellow A4 pad, occasionally stopping to clarify a point. When I had finished, she put down her black gel pen, and said, 'well, that seems straightforward. Let's tell them we're ready. Oh, and don't say anything unless I tell you.'

We had to wait for half an hour while the station found a free interview room and both the police officers involved. Finally, we were all sat around a large table. Anita and I were on one side, DS Penry and DC Rushton on the other, all of us sat on blue plastic chairs with metal legs that could stack easily.

DC Rushton put two new CDs into a black machine at one end of the table, and hit a record button. He began by reciting where we were, the date and time, and his own name. Then, just like on the police shows, we all had to give our own name. I was surprised when I also had to give, not only my address, but also my date of birth and national insurance number. DC Rushton then cautioned me, told me that I was not under arrest, and free to go, and that he wouldn't be using his s.20 powers. I felt stupid for not knowing what s.20 powers were, so even more stupidly didn't ask.

The interview did not go as I expected.

DC Rushton began.

'So, Mister Andrews, could you please tell us why you stole the papyrus found in your rucksack yesterday?'

Before I could answer, Anita intervened.

'I'm so sorry, but it's Doctor Andrews. Could we please show some courtesy towards my client?'

DC Rushton sighed quietly; DS Penry started rolling her eyes, caught herself, straightened up and smiled.

'Of course, our apologies. Doctor Andrews', she continued, emphasising the doctor, 'could you provide us with an explanation?'

Again, Anita replied before I could say anything.

'Could I just check why you're asking? Only, this papyrus isn't missing, and isn't connected to any crime, is it? And, if I'm not mistaken...', here she paused, flipping through the papers before stopping at one and peering at it intently, 'this papyrus wasn't stolen. I mean, you found it in the museum. It hadn't left the John Rylands. In fact, it hadn't even left my client's office. To accuse my client of theft in such circumstances seems like...', again she paused, looking around her as if to find something to compare with, '... accusing someone of shoplifting when they put a tin of soup in their shopping trolley in Waitrose.' Here, she looked directly at DC Rushton. 'Or Lidl.'

Anita was turning out to have a mean streak. DC Rushton's eyes narrowed slightly, and he tightened his mouth. DS Penry intervened.

'I like Lidl. Always "Lidl on price", isn't that their slogan?'

Anita turned to her, and smiled.

'I'm sure it is. But you must see the issue. Why on earth are you interviewing my client about a scrap of papyrus that isn't worth much, that has no forensics linking it to him, that in any case he has a right to handle, and that never left his office? If this is all you want to ask him about, I think we need to end the interview here.'

DC Rushton looked sideways at DS Penry, and shrugged. She looked back, nodded, and then turned to us again.

'Okay, we'll leave the papyri piece found in your ruck-sack, though we still consider it evidence that might be material to the disappearance of the other papyri piece.'

I decided that now was not the time to educate her about papyrus being the singular, and papyri the plural.

Anita clearly disagreed with my assessment.

'I think you mean papyrus. Unless you are accusing my client of taking multiple papyri?'

DC Penry smiled, but behind her eyes winter had arrived. She pointedly turned her gaze away from my solicitor, and locked eyes with me.

'Doctor Andrews, please could you give your account of the events of yesterday?'

I looked across at Anita, who shrugged, then said, 'You can answer that'.

My cheeks felt red, as I started to narrate what had happened, conscious of an audience not only of the police, but also the recording. I wondered who else would get to hear it.

Once I had finished, DS Penry began checking details. Had I seen anyone by the desk, picking anything up? Was I sure I had locked my room? Who else had keys? How could I know what time I had returned? And others.

Then the questioning took a more personal turn.

'Doctor Andrews, are you in financial difficulties?'

I am a post-doc desperately trying to find a succession of temporary jobs until I find one that is tenure-track and gain a permanent contract with a university or institute. The work is low paid and in some of my previous roles the contract hadn't covered the holidays, leaving me to fend for myself. I had three degrees, all of which had needed loans to fund them. Of course I was in financial difficulties. So was everyone in my situation.

'I'm getting by,' I replied, cautiously.

'It's just that you would seem to be the obvious suspect. You have the means to steal the papyrus, as you work at the John Rylands Library. You certainly had the opportunity. And the money you might make from selling it would bail you out of money troubles. Means, motive, opportunity.'

I stayed silent. DS Penry continued.

'In your professional opinion, Doctor Andrews, how much might your fragment be worth? How important is it?'

The events of the morning had already given me the lower limit of what it was worth at one hundred thousand dollars. I decided not to share this information.

'Impossible to say. If it is confirmed as genuine, the fragment is unique. It would be the earliest physical evidence of the Jesus tradition, earlier even than optimistic datings for P52. That alone makes it priceless. But also, it would be evidence of a different Christian tradition right from the start. Put the two together...' I shrugged my shoulders.

DC Rushton asked, 'P52?'

'A scrap of John's gospel owned by the John Rylands. Some scholarship dates it to the beginning of the second century. This fragment would be fifty or so years earlier.'

DS Penry pulled her chair a little closer to the table, straightened up, and asked directly, 'Doctor Andrews, did you take the missing papyrus?'

Anita started telling me not to answer, but I cut across her.

'No, I didn't. And I don't know who did.'

'Okay, Doctor Andrews, thank you for your time. For

now, you're free to go. Here's a card with my number on and the case id if you should remember any useful information.'

'He was always free to go. This is a voluntary interview that my client gave as he wishes to help the police as much as possible.'

Anita clearly liked to get the last word.

Chapter Fourteen

B y the time I left the police station, it was lunchtime,
and my stomach had begun rumbling in anticipa-
tion. I walked down Oldham Road towards the
Northern Quarter, where I found a café near the Craft
Centre. I opted for a fish-finger ciabatta, which almost but
not quite worked as a combination. The sandwich did
manage to fill me up, washed down with a cappuccino that
was almost but not quite strong enough. The slight disappointment of the meal reminded me of my bigger problems,
and I wondered if I would be able to afford many café visits
in the months ahead.

I shook my head, wanting to clear it of such thoughts. I
had spent long enough feeling sorry for myself. It was time to
be active. I sat back in my chair and wondered what to do
with the rest of the day.

At that point I remembered that my door was still
broken, and started googling locksmiths, and texting my landlord. I found repairs happened quicker if I sorted out all the

practical details first, then presented both the problem and solution to my landlord in one go.

Sure enough, once I established a quote and a promise of immediate action from one contact, the landlord gave the go-ahead. That also settled what I was going to do with the rest of the day; go home and wait for the locksmith to arrive.

I strolled back past the goth magnet of Afflecks Palace, making my way towards Piccadilly Gardens. At this time of year, midweek, there weren't too many people on the grass: a handful of couples; two or three parents with young children; and a few souls determinedly drinking their way through cans of lager.

When I got to the bus station, I popped into the nearby mini supermarket for some greens for Mister B., and some chocolate (Galaxy), bread and milk for myself. Then I added a smoothie. If I could be bothered to buy healthy food for a rabbit, I could do it for myself. But I didn't put back the chocolate.

I didn't have to wait long for the bus, and climbed up the stairs to take a seat at the front. As it began to rattle its way through the streets of south Manchester, my mind turned back to Brad Ryan. Who could he be working for? Although I was generally aware of the murky trades in biblical arte-facts, it wasn't my area of expertise. Maisy, on the other hand, had written a couple of blog posts, presented at a conference, and contributed to a couple of newspaper articles in America recently on the topic. I texted her.

Can we chat sometime? Need to pick your brains.

The reply came within a couple of minutes.

Come round for dinner tonight. You could do with some tlc anyway. 7.30pm

I smiled. At least I could look forward to the evening.

I looked up from the phone; the bus was making its way through the curry mile (in fact closer to about two-thirds of a mile, and now as many middle eastern outlets as Asian restaurants, but the banners still said 'Curry Mile'). I was nearly at my stop. A couple of minutes later I pressed the bell and moved back down the stairs.

The bus pulled into the stop, and the doors started to swing open. As I thanked the driver, my phone started ringing.

I looked at the screen to check who was calling, and then sighed. This was not a call I was ready to take.

It was my mother.

Chapter Fifteen

'Hi mum, how are you?'

'We're fine. But I'm not calling about us. What have you got yourself involved in?'

I paused, surprised. I didn't think my parents read the Manchester Evening Standard. I opted for caution.

'What are you talking about?'

'They're saying you stole a piece of the Bible. Why would you do that?'

My mother managed to sound both offended and angry, as if my misdemeanours were aimed at her.

'I didn't. Where are you getting this info from?'

'It's all over the internet. Your dad saw it first. We brought you up better than this. If you were struggling, you could have asked.'

'I haven't stolen anything, but thanks for the vote of confidence.'

'Well, the papers say you have. Why would they lie?'

'Look, it's a misunderstanding. I... the museum has

mislaid an old copy of a small part of a gospel. I'm not under arrest, and I haven't done anything wrong.'

My mother sniffed.

'Well, that's not what the papers are saying. What gospel?'

'The gospel of Mary Magdalene.'

'The prostitute? That's not even a proper gospel. And who would name a gospel after her?'

I sighed inwardly. My mother had never paid much attention to my research.

'There's no evidence that Mary Magdalene was a prostitute. You can blame Gregory the Great for that theory. And there's lots of not-proper gospels. This is one of them.'

'No, she was a prostitute. Read the proper gospels. I don't know this Gregory, but he's right.'

There are times in life when you have to decide whether the effort is worth it. For this argument, as with so many involving my mother, I had reached my limit. And I was also itching to check which national papers had picked up the story. I changed tack.

'Have you told Mrs Barswell that your son is in all the papers?'

A slight pause told me that this was an angle that had not yet occurred to my mother. Mrs Barswell was her neighbour, her friend, and her rival in the great game of life.

My mother replied, 'I don't think Adam has been in the papers at all. Certainly not the nationals.' Adam was Mrs Barswell's son, who was a similar age to me. I decided to press home my advantage.

'I am dealing with unique, priceless objects that are of major historical importance. In a way, it's not surprising the press are interested.'

'Yes, far more interesting than being a lawyer.'

I could hear a lighter tone in my mother's voice, and wondered how long it would be before she would be in Mrs Barswell's kitchen, sipping a mug of tea and finding ways to emphasise the new-found fame of her son the doctor. It turned out to be not very long at all.

'You've reminded me, I've got a tray that I need to return to Anne. I might pop round and drop it off. See what Adam's up to these days.'

'Good idea. I'm sure you've got lots to catch up on.'

'And any romantic news to pass on? You're not getting any younger. And neither are we.'

My mother was desperate for grandchildren to dote on.

'No, nothing to report.'

'What about that Daisy you work with. She seems like a nice girl. Why don't you ask her out for a coffee? Or buy her some flowers. Show her you're interested.'

'It's Maisy. And I'm not her type. Look, I've got to go now. Bye mum.'

By the time the conversation had (thankfully) ended, I was nearly back home. I started paying attention to my surroundings again. Somewhere, from a window, floated the sound of a clarinet channelling Mozart. Some Royal Northern College of Music student was probably practising for their exams. A black and white cat looked furtively around, and then dashed across the street, missing by a few seconds the arrival of a black car with tinted windows. A white transit van, grubby with dust, was parked directly outside my house, passenger-side wheels on the pavement.

I slowed down, then stopped. I had never seen that van before, and I didn't fancy meeting the people who had broken into my house.

Both doors opened. On the driver's side, out came a large man with muscles bursting out of a black t-shirt and wearing jeans decorated with oil and sawdust. On the passenger's side, a younger man, maybe just out of his teens, emerged with a slighter build, and sporting an attempt at a moustache.

The bigger, older man looked at me.

'I've been expecting you.'

Chapter Sixteen

'Any sugar?'

The van had belonged to Dave, the locksmith. He had arrived earlier than expected, another job having been cancelled, and so I was making mugs of tea as a contribution to his practical skills.

'Two for me, none for the lad, milk in both.'

The lad was Dave's helper, his nephew Gavin.

The kettle started gurgling away and blowing steam across the counter while I reached over to flick the switch and turn it off. It was meant to do this automatically, but was now forgetful in its old age. Pete had told me three months ago that he would buy a new one.

Pete often tells people things he is going to do. Sometimes, he does.

I found a couple of clean mugs in the cupboard; one celebrating the 2012 Commonwealth Games, and one with a picture of a faded cartoon penguin. I tossed a teabag in each, added sugar to the Commonwealth Games mug, and poured in the water.

The milk was beyond its sell-by date, but passed the sniff test, so I topped up the mugs, squashed a bit more flavour out of the teabags with a teaspoon, and handed over them over.

This task complete, I retreated to my study, sat back in my office chair, and tried to order my thoughts as the noise of a drill vibrated through the house. I decided the first step was to see what my mother had been talking about.

I took out my phone and searched through the websites of a range of national tabloids. I wasn't the main story, but it didn't take too long to find it either. The national papers had gone more full-blooded than the local, implying strongly that I might be a suspect and playing up the lost gospel aspect to the hilt. One enterprising journalist had even managed to get a quote out of Dan Brown. At least, I thought that until I noticed that that journalist also had direct quotes from a number of people involved, including me, that had clearly been made up.

Two of the papers had published photos of me. It looked like they had taken them off Instagram or Facebook, though not from my feed. I was at a party, drink in hand, with an awkward smile. I tried to decide if that made me look more or less guilty, before putting the phone down and sighing. It was going to be a long few days.

There was a light knock on the room door.

'Do you mind if I use your loo?'

It was Gavin. I directed him up the stairs. Meanwhile, Dave came through the hall to the kitchen, brandishing two mugs.

'Finished these – thanks. Appreciated. I never say no to tea. So, are you a student?'

'No, I work at the John Rylands on Deansgate looking after papyri.'

'Oh, I made that in primary school. We made like a lattice out of strips of brown paper and PVA glue, and then wrote hieroglyphics. So can you read them?'

'My papyri were written in Greek.'

'Oh.' Dave sounded a little disappointed. Then his face brightened. 'Still, it's all Greek to me. Bet you've never heard that one before. We went there last year, one of the islands. Got sunburnt badly.'

I placed the mugs in the sink, promising to myself that I would remember to wash them later and not abandon them.

'Anyway, all done – we've finished. Come and have a look.'

The locksmith showed me the new lock on the door, and started to explain its benefits over the old lock. I politely nodded my head and pretended to understand (and care about) what he was saying. He also explained how he had strengthened the door. It ended with Dave giving me two keys, and I gave him the landlord's details for the invoice.

'Don't you have individual locks on the bedrooms?' he asked.

'No. It was originally just a family house, but the landlord moved away and started renting it out. Also, he said something about not being able to have locks because of fire regulations or something.'

The locksmith pursed his lips dubiously. 'I think he's got that wrong. If you want a lock fitted on those bedroom doors, come back to me.'

I wondered briefly how much the locks would have helped, or whether he would now be repairing three doors instead of one.

Once Dave and Gavin had gone, I returned to the sink. Since I had more time on my hands, I decided I may as well keep the place tidy. In a couple of minutes, the mugs were clean and on the draining board.

Thump.

Mr B was getting restless again. I checked his water and threw in a bit more hay. That seemed to settle him down, and he started nibbling the fresh pile.

The house suddenly felt quiet. All I could hear was a background hum of traffic. And I had nothing to do, and no-one to be with. The harsh reality of my situation started to seep out from dark recesses of my mind into the open.

'Just you and me, then,' I said to Mr B. He looked up briefly, head slightly tilted to one side quizzically, sniffed a couple of times, and returned to his hay. He wasn't much of a conversation partner.

I began to wonder what might come next, and came up with nothing. If there was a future ahead, it was playing hide and seek with me, and winning.

This was doing me no favours. I tried to shake myself out of my worries, by wandering through to my study. At least tidying up offered the possibility of some distraction. I put on some Oasis and got to work.

It did not take long. I was shuffling a final pile of paper notes when my phone beeped. It was Maisy.

Remember tonite pbab

I returned to the kitchen to check if we had any wine I could take. All I could find was a bottle of cheap port that was only a quarter full. I had vague memories of Pete opening it around Christmas time. Maisy appreciated good wine; I was pretty sure that the port wouldn't qualify. I would have to go out to the corner shop and find something more suitable. I checked my pockets for spare cash, but only found a collection of business cards people had given me during the day. I dumped them on the work surface top and sighed. Another expense for the credit card.

I glanced at the time on my phone. I had about an hour before I needed to leave. Briefly I thought about another shower and smart clothes, but Maisy was an old friend, not only a colleague. I didn't need to make an effort with her. Instead, I used the time productively by flopping onto the sofa, turning on the TV, and watching a couple of episodes of *Gavin and Stacey* on BBC iPlayer.

It kept me from dwelling on my misfortunes until it was time to go to Maisy's. I grabbed my coat, and walked out of the door, checking that the new lock was working properly. The last thing I needed was to find I couldn't get back inside the house because the key stuck.

But Dave and Gavin had done their job well. The key turned silkily smooth, gliding rather than clunking.

Time to get the wine. I headed towards the main road. The side road was quiet. No cars, no vans moving around.

Once I reached Wilmslow Road, I entered New Zealand Wines, pondering no doubt like many before me the process involved in choosing that name for a store. I finally settled on a red pinot noir, at £7.99, before using my phone to arrange an Uber to Maisy's. A car was one minute away.

I went back to the main road to look out for the car, watching the buses and other traffic trundling past. Almost instantly, I saw my ride, a silver Toyota Corolla, just behind a red Fiat Panda and just in front of a black Audi with tinted windows.

I got in the Corolla, checking that the driver had the right address, and we set off for Maisy's.

As we started to navigate the traffic on Wilmslow Road, a thought kept niggling at me. Hadn't I seen that black car earlier?

Chapter Seventeen

'Jake! Come in!'

Regina held open the front door, a typically enthusiastic smile accompanying her exuberant welcome. I stepped inside, offering the bottle of Pinot Noir as I did.

'Hi Regina, you look lovely as always. And I'm liking the dress; very smart.'

Regina glanced down at herself. A burgundy silk dress shimmered in the lights, matching shoes with heels pointed enough to qualify as lethal weapons.

'Well, it's nice to dress up for dinner parties.' At this point Regina looked briefly at what I was wearing. 'But not obligatory. Come on through and meet the others.'

Maisy hadn't told me that this was going to be a dinner party. I had assumed it was going to be a takeaway with Maisy and her wife. I could feel my cheeks going slightly red as I regretted my earlier decision to binge TV rather than get changed into smarter clothes.

We walked through the long, narrow, Victorian hallway

past a couple of rooms into a large kitchen at the back of the house. A red Le Creuset pot was burbling away, intermittently releasing scents of lamb and coriander as a small blue flame kept it simmering on the hob on the left of the room. On the right of the room, four people were sitting around a large pine table, drinking red wine. The table already had cutlery set out, and a thick candle shed flickering light, bolstered by uplighters in the corners of the room. I only recognised Maisy out of the four.

'Jake, sit down. This is Jake, everybody.'

The only spaces left were at either end of the table. I sat down on a heavy wooden chair and pulled it closer to the table. The weight made it scrape along, leaving me worried that I might have scratched the floor. I decided looking down would be too obvious, so I smiled brightly and reached for one of the empty glasses on the table. Regina left me and went to tending over the food.

On my right was a thin man with a thin moustache, dressed with suit and thin navy tie, intently examining a fork. Next to him sat a woman with a navy maxi dress and dark, long hair. The woman introduced herself.

'Hello, I'm Agnieszka, and this is Pietr, my partner.'

This was said with a smile. Pietr looked up at me, and allowed a brief acknowledgement to flit across his face before returning to what seemed to be a careful examination of how clean the fork was.

'And I'm Molly; good to meet you.'

This was from the person to my left. Erratic dark brown hair framed a face with a wide smile and twinkling eyes. Also, I noticed, she was wearing a long, shapeless, green jumper with a hole at one elbow, matched with black leggings and Doc Martens. Inwardly I could feel a little tension dissipate; at least I wouldn't be the only person who didn't dress up.

Maisy continued the introductions.

'Agniezska works with Regina at CIC. And Pietr also works there – funny story how they met. And Molly is my cousin who's just moved to Manchester.'

Molly smiled at me, picked up the open bottle of red, and poured a glass for me.

'Molly's in AV stuff. And this is Jake, who's my colleague.'

'For now, right?' Pietr involved himself in the conversation. Unhelpfully.

Small grimaces of discomfort and embarrassment flicked on and off the others' faces.

'Hopefully for a long time. Don't believe everything you read in the papers.' I tried to appear bright and cheerful.

'So it isn't true? You haven't lost an important papyrus and been suspended?' Pietr ploughed on, oblivious to the darkening atmosphere in the room.

'No, that is true.' I sighed, but Regina was already coming to the rescue.

'Get ready,' she called out, 'first course coming up. Maisy, can you come and help? Anyone allergic to fish?'

'Won't your organisation let you go? That's what would happen at CIC if I made a massive mistake.'

I could see why Pietr had opted for industry rather than the diplomatic corps.

Molly intervened, much to my relief.

'What does CIC stand for? And what do you actually do? Oh, mackerel pâté. Lovely. Thanks, Regina.'

I took a sip of the red. Smooth scents of raspberries and

mushrooms, with hints of vanilla, began to dance about my mouth. This wine was far better than my contribution.

Agnieszka replied to Molly. 'CIC is Chemicals International Company, but everybody just uses the initials. We sell pharmaceuticals. Medicines and so on.'

The conversation stayed safely away from papyri as we munched and crunched our way through the pâté on sourdough toast, followed by a lamb tagine with couscous.

But as Maisy brought out the puddings–individual lemon and blueberry tarts–I came under focus again.

'Jake, how worried are you about your job?' asked Agnieszka. As Maisy was sitting down, she raised her eyebrows at me, offering me a chance for the topic to be changed again. I made a slight shake of the head at her, then replied.

'If I'm honest, really worried. Like, really. Someone else took the fragment, but I'm going to cop the blame.'

Pietr chipped in. 'Then you must find out how that person was. Then you will not get the blame.'

'Yes, who do you think it was?' asked Molly. She smiled, then in a loud stage whisper announced, 'Perhaps Maisy has the fragment, and is going to sell it and spend all the money on wine'. Maisy rolled her eyes and ostentatiously poured herself another glass of red. I smiled and replied to Molly.

'We had a group in on the Monday. One of them has been sniffing around seeing if I can sell him the fragment. Brad Ryan. Do you know anything about him, Maisy?'

'Keep away. He's trouble. There's a lot of murky trades in the antiquities world, and Ryan's recently often been found down in the dirt. Money to burn, and no scruples, no questions asked.'

'He mentioned some collector, doing a Museum of the Bible copy?'

'Yes, but I don't know the name of the collector. Ryan probably gets paid a lot for discretion, so that his client can keep his nose clean officially. American, and rich. That's all I know.'

Molly joined in again. 'Anyway, it can't be him, because he wants to buy the thing. So it has to be one of the others.'

I nodded my agreement.

'It must be one of them. This Catholic priest was digging around and asking lots of questions. Maybe him?'

'How very Da Vinci Code. It's the Vatican trying to shut down a new gospel,' said Regina, jokingly. But Pietr's eyes lit up, and he sat up straight.

'Yes, yes, that makes sense. Find him. That is your task.'

I shifted a little uneasily in my seat. 'My task?'

'Yes.' Pietr was emphatic. 'You must show it is him.'

'Isn't this a job for the police?' said Molly.

Pietr was already shaking his head before the words had finished leaving her mouth. 'No. The police have their suspect.'

Maisy leaned back in her chair, looking up to the ceiling with eyes squinting. 'He's right. The police don't have time to investigate properly. And, let's face it, you've nothing better to do tomorrow. Check out the priest.'

I began to feel a little flushed again, not helped by the wine I had been drinking. Everyone seemed to want me to play amateur detective.

'There's one minor little detail that you're all missing,' I replied. 'I have no leads on the priest. He could be staying anywhere in Manchester. How can I check him out?'

Maisy leaned forward. She said slowly and clearly, 'I know where he's staying.'

Chapter Eighteen

We all turned to look at Maisy. I asked the obvious question.

'How? And, now I think about it, why?'

'I met him at his hotel last week. Friday afternoon.'

Regina chipped in. 'Oh, that was him. You said you had a meeting.'

'Let me get this straight,' I said. 'You have met the priest, whatsisname, at his hotel. Why?'

Maisy had looked down to fiddle with her phone.

'Augusto Zappacosta,' she announced, triumphantly. 'He asked for a meeting. He phoned up, said he wanted to talk papyri, and suggested afternoon tea in the hotel lounge as a meeting point. Nice scones.'

'And did he? Want to talk about papyri?' asked Molly.

By this time Maisy had put a spoonful of tart in her mouth. She nodded, and then started speaking, with the occasional crumb falling out. 'The rare ones. Not just P52, but also P6. That's pretty specialised. Augusto knows his stuff.'

'I thought we'd lent that to the British Museum?'

Maisy shook her head. 'We've got it back. He seemed to be obsessed about the oldest or first of anything.'

'So?' I asked.

'So what?' said Maisy, confused.

''Which hotel? Where is he staying?'

'The Prince Edward. It's just outside Chinatown. It's not the Midland, but it's okay. Like I said, nice scones.'

Regina said, 'the best scones are at Sugar Junction.'

Pietr started shaking his head. 'No, the Richmond Tea Rooms. You get a better choice, and they aren't as heavy.'

Agnieszka stopped chewing a mouthful of tart to agree, 'Richmond is fab. We went there when my mother came over.'

I could feel the conversation spiralling away.

'So he's at the Prince Edward. What am I meant to do next? Pretend I'm a private detective?'

To my surprise, Molly took this suggestion seriously. Her face lit up.

'Ooh, I've always wanted to do this. We could follow him about hiding behind newspapers and see what nefarious deeds he gets up to.' Perhaps Molly was not so much serious as enthusiastic.

Maisy rolled her eyes again. 'Nefarious. He's a priest. He'll probably go to mass.'

'Still, it would be fun trying. You up for it?' Molly looked at me.

I took a moment to respond, taken aback both by the prospect of trying to trail a priest around town, and by doing it in the company of Molly. Before I could reply, Maisy stepped in.

'Or you could sit in your house, watching *Cash in the Attic*, and feeling sorry for yourself.'

'But I like *Cash in the Attic*,' I said weakly.

Maisy looked at me sardonically. Pietr began shaking his head, and said, 'Leave this to the authorities. Don't meddle,' which confused me, because he had been saying the opposite a few moments ago. But Agnieszka grinned, and said to him, 'He can't do any harm. He's only going to follow him around. What's the worst that could happen?'

Regina nodded, and said, 'If I did nothing, it would drive me crazy. Better to be active and doing something. And', she turned to Maisy at this point, 'if I ever choose *Cash in the Attic* over anything else, shoot me.'

I gave in to peer pressure.

'Okay, I'll turn up there tomorrow morning. Do I need to buy a deerstalker?'

Pietr perked up. 'Ah, a Sherlock Holmes reference. Very funny. But the deerstalker is not mentioned by name in the books.'

'Is it a film thing, then,' asked Regina.

'No, it's the illustrator, Paget. He drew him in a deerstalker,' I said. I got a look of admiration from Pietr for offering this factoid, and a tilt of the head from Regina in acknowledgement of the answer. Maisy and Molly had ignored the exchange.

'What time shall we meet?' Molly asked. So she was serious about joining me.

'What about your job? Won't they mind?' I asked.

'I don't start until next Monday. Doing maternity cover in a school's external relations department.'

'Nine o'clock okay?'

'It's a date,' Molly replied. And smiled.

Chapter Nineteen

There was a steady trickle of earnest young men in dark suits and bright ties coming into the hotel, on occasions blocking my view of the reception desk. I shifted a little on the tangerine-coloured sofa in the large, soulless bar area, trying to get a clearer angle. The hotel was hosting a conference on '5G Networks and AI: a proactive approach for business'. It made me feel better about rejecting a corporate career.

I checked my phone again. It was still five minutes before Molly and I had agreed to meet. I had come much earlier, at 7.30am. This owed as much to not being able to sleep as it did to diligence. Half the night had been spent wondering what my future life might look like if the papyrus stayed missing, and half puzzling over what exactly Molly had meant by, 'It's a date'. I had not seen the priest since my arrival, and I was wondering if he was still staying at the hotel.

Molly strode through the front glass doors, in a navy suit with white blouse, carrying a newspaper. Her hair was neatly tidied away in a ponytail. She spotted me, waved and came over, sitting on an armchair next to the sofa.

'You look a bit smarter than yesterday,' she said. 'I was wondering if you were one of those people who are always a bit scruffy.'

'Funny, I was wondering the same about you.'

'I've got our detective equipment,' she said smiling, and opened up the newspaper. It was a copy of the Daily Telegraph with two holes cut out to look through. She held it up close to her face, peering through the holes mischievously.

'Thanks. I'm sure that won't draw any attention to us at all,' I responded. 'Coffee?'

'Who are you talking to? I'm invisible.'

'Americano? Milk and sugar on the side?' Molly nodded, still holding the newspaper to her face, so the whole of it bobbed up and down.

I stood up, and made my way to the bar. As I did, the lift doors on the other side of the lobby slid apart, and Father Augusto stepped out. He was again dressed in clerical black and carrying a small leather briefcase. He strode to the reception desk, smiled and nodded at the staff, and handed over his room key. Then, he walked out of the hotel, pausing on the pavement outside, perhaps adjusting to the bright sunshine.

I returned to Molly, trying to balance speed with being inconspicuous.

'No time for coffee; that's him.'

'Let's go.' Molly stood up, folded up the paper, and we walked closer to the exit, staying inside the hotel. Outside, Father Augusto held up his phone, then glanced at the buildings around him. It looked like he was consulting a map app. He looked at his phone again, and headed off to the right of the hotel.

'Good thing he didn't get an Uber. What was your plan going to be?'

I shrugged. 'Hope for another taxi, hop in, and finally be able to say, "follow that car!"'

I pushed open the large glass door, and we walked out onto the street. Father Augusto was about seventy yards away from us, making his way down the street confidently towards the next crossroads. Molly and I kept up our pursuit, feeling self-conscious and a little foolish. At least, I was. Molly seemed to be enjoying it, judging by her smile.

At the crossroads, Father Augusto waited for the lights, crossed and then turned right. By the time we reached the junction, the lights had changed again, and we had to wait.

'Don't let him get away!' Molly said.

'What? He isn't. We can still see him, and he's only walking,' I replied.

'I know. But I've always wanted to say that. Makes it sound more exciting. You know, like "follow that car" that you were talking about.'

'Oh... yes'. My cheeks reddened slightly at my misunderstanding.

'Green man. Thunderbirds are go!'

'Never watched it,' I said, as we crossed the road.

'Poor deprived soul. Hold on, he's turned off the main road.'

I was about to reply, but a white van accelerated past, belching out dark fumes that caught the back of my throat. I coughed instead. Molly increased her pace as I struggled to breath and to keep up.

The road down which Father Augusto had turned would never, even by the most optimistic estate agent, be called salubrious. The buildings lining the left-hand side were a mix of old red Victorian brick warehouses with serious neglect since the time of the industrial revolution and sad, drab, concrete-clad workshops that had seen their heyday in the nineteen sixties. On the right side of the road was a series of mostly bricked up railway arches. Green strands emerged from cracks in walls and bricks; nature seeking to reclaim lost territory. Most of the windows were boarded up; those that weren't were broken. An industrial-sized grey rubbish bin blocked the pavement on the left, overflowing with ripped black refuse sacks, random detritus and smells of dust and rancid food. This was part of Manchester visitors rarely came across: unregenerated, unloved and uninspiring.

It seemed an unlikely tourist destination for a Catholic priest from Italy.

Father Augusto was still ahead of us, but he had come to a stop where a narrow alley on the left-hand side met the road. He looked down the alley, smiled and waved.

Molly and I glanced at each other, both puzzled. This was not how I had expected the day to go. To be honest, my expectations were that we would not even see the priest, and that it would be a waste of time. But I certainly didn't expect to end up in Manchester's underbelly.

Our surprise increased when the person whom Father Augusto had greeted emerged from the shadows of the alley.

It was a woman. A woman in a burgundy leather miniskirt so short that it could have been sold as a belt without breaking the Trades Description Act. The skirt was paired with strappy high heels and a black spaghetti strap top. She had bright blonde hair with some dark roots showing.

Father Augusto and the woman embraced, then she led him back into the alley.

'I don't like to make assumptions...' I said.

'I do. We're near Manchester's red-light district here. I don't think Father Augusto is a very good priest. So what do we do now, Sherlock?'

'Let's walk past the end of the alley. We don't want to lose him, and they might be going somewhere else.'

We began to walk down the depressed road, past the bin, towards the alley crossing. Low, deep, rumbles echoed around from nearby railway tracks above the walled-up arches. We were near Piccadilly Station.

As we neared the alley, we whispered a plan to one another.

'I'll go on your right,' I said. 'As we walk past, I'll look at you, and so I'll be looking in the direction of the alley. We can pretend to be talking.'

'We are talking,' Molly replied, 'and I need to go on the right. You've met him; if he sees you looking at him that would be beyond weird for him. He doesn't know me.'

I shrugged, and moved to her left, and we continued walking.

'I don't think I heard last night what you do in AV, or where the school is you're going to be working for.'

We were now crossing the alley. I was looking at Molly, and she was looking past me into its shadows.

'There's no-one there.'

Chapter Twenty

I whirled around. Father Augusto and the woman had vanished.

'They must have walked through to the next road,' I said. 'We'd better make sure we don't lose them.'

Molly and I made our way down the alley, picking our way past discarded cans and dog dirt, though failing to escape the smell. The alley was just over a car-width wide, with faded yellow lines on both sides. It was about fifty yards long, ending where it met a larger road again. Either side, the tall brick buildings made it seem like a dark red canyon, blocking out much of the light.

'This is less glamorous than I thought it might be,' said Molly. 'This area's rough.'

'Welcome to the mean streets of Manchester. Nothing that can faze a hard-boiled private eye,' I said.

'I see we've moved on from Conan Doyle to 1940s Raymond Chandler,' said Molly.

'Both great detective writers,' I said, checking my shoe to

make sure I hadn't stepped in anything. 'Though these buildings are more Victorian warehouse than 1940s.'

We reached the end of the alley, and looked left and right down the road it had led to. A woman dressed in a blue tracksuit came towards us, steering a pushchair with one hand and holding a mobile with the other. She was haranguing someone (it sounded like it must be her partner) on the phone. In the pushchair, a bored toddler was slumped to one side, picking his nose and staring at us.

Apart from the woman, the pavements were empty. There was no sign of either the priest or the woman with blonde hair.

'Curiouser and curiouser,' said Molly.

'There's nowhere they could have gone here. We'd see them,' I said.

'Then they must have entered a building from the alleyway.'

'I suppose so. I didn't see a doorway, but I was concentrating on not stepping on dog dirt.'

'It was the vomit over the discarded chips that I was avoiding,' said Molly. 'Anyway, when you have eliminated the impossible, whatever remains, however improbable, must be the truth.'

'Now who's Sherlock.'

We turned back into the alley, and started down it, this time looking for doors and again checking our steps carefully. On my left, a large black plastic bag was spilling its contents over the ground. Then, the inside of the bag started rustling and moving, and something small and grey darted out, then back in. I shuddered, and moved on.

And, about halfway down the alley, on the right-hand side, a couple of grey concrete steps led to a wooden door set in the side of what would once have been a thriving Victorian storage depot. It had long ago been painted a dark blue, but over time this had bleached and started to peel away, revealing pale bare wood.

'I think we've found the right place,' I whispered to Molly.

In the centre of the door was a small, slate-grey plaque, screwed into the wood. In neat white letters, the sign read, 'The Magdalene Initiative'.

Chapter Twenty-One

Molly and I both stared at the door.

'Have you heard of the Magdalene Initiative', she asked.

'No.'

'Well, Google is our friend.' She whipped out her phone, and started typing. 'Or maybe not so friendly. Nothing relevant on the internet.'

I wondered what groups nowadays had no web presence. Molly voiced my fears.

'Do you think it's a weird cult thing?' she whispered.

I shrugged my shoulders, noticing my own matching reticence to make a noise.

'Well, we could knock, but that might be awkward,' I said. 'We can hardly claim we got lost.'

'I think we're being watched,' Molly said, and pointed above the door. Screwed into the brick was a small black plate, holding up a small camera, also in black. Underneath the camera, a dim blue LED light flashed.

'Time to go,' I said, turning away and checking my path for possible dog dirt.

'Too late,' Molly replied.

The door opened towards us, the creaking hinges doing nothing to allay anxiety.

Behind it was a short lady who instantly gave off mothering vibes.

'Hello, hello, come in. Sorry about the buzzer. We've been waiting for two months now for it to be fixed. But at least I spotted you. You'll be wanting a cup of tea before we start. Follow me.' She smiled, turned around and walked confidently away from us down a magnolia-painted corridor with well-worn blue linoleum flooring. She was clearly expecting us both to follow.

Molly looked over at me, shrugged, and stepped inside. I mentally sighed, and followed after Molly.

'I'm Janet,' the woman called behind her, as she led us through a door on the left into a larger room, about thirty feet square.

I looked around. The walls were painted magnolia like the corridor, but the flooring changed to dark green industrial carpet tiles. In the far right-hand corner, two tiles were missing, revealing a bare concrete floor. The windows were tall and narrow, made of frosted glass with protective wire outside them. This hadn't prevented a smash in the window on the far left, enabling rumbles from the railway to provide a low bass accompaniment. In the centre of the room was a wooden coffee table, stained from too many mugs and too few coasters, operating in the no-man's land between smartly new and gracefully antique. Clustered around the table were two sofas and an armchair, all in plain, faded navy. Ancient stains provided some patterning. The left armrest on the armchair was ripped, and yellow foam was pressing outwards, as though making a bid for freedom. Everything smelled slightly of dust.

'Come and sit down, and I'll get you sorted with drinks. Tea and biscuits.' Janet gestured towards the seating, smiled again, and bustled out of the door, closing it behind her, leaving Molly and me alone.

It appeared to be a day for shrugs. We both shrugged at each other, and sat down, Molly on the armchair while I chose the sofa to its left, giving me a view of the doorway.

'What's going on?' I whispered.

'If this is a cult, it's not what I expected from cults. I thought they would be a bit more slick and modern, not tea and crumpets.'

'Biscuits.'

'What?'

'We were promised tea and biscuits, not tea and crumpets.'

'Does that make it any more cult-like?'

'I don't know,' I replied. 'It's not how I imagined a brothel, either.'

Molly got up, walked to the door, opened it a fraction, closed it again, and returned to sit down.

'Just wanted to make sure we weren't locked in,' she explained.

Footsteps sounded from the corridor, getting louder. The door opened and Janet entered, carrying a tray with two mugs with a teaspoon sticking out of each, a green plate with four digestive biscuits on it, a small stainless-steel bowl, and a stainless-steel jug. She placed the tray onto the coffee table.

'Here you go. Help yourself to milk and sugar. And biscuits. No chocolate ones today, I'm afraid. You're a bit early. The others won't be arriving for another ten minutes or so.' Another smile – she seemed to be genuinely pleased we had come – and then she left us again.

I leant forward, and poured some milk into one of the mugs, and some milk onto the tray as it ran down the spout. I wondered if people who designed metal jugs ever tried to use them. I looked over at Molly, and raised my eyebrows questioningly. She nodded, and I added some milk to hers, more successfully now the jug was emptier.

'Sugar?'

'Sweet enough.'

I stirred both mugs, and handed one to Molly. Mine celebrated St Mary's Primary School 1989. Molly's declared 'Ban the Bomb'. If this was a cult, it wasn't a rich one, but it had been around for a while.

More footsteps. Janet reappeared. 'Have a biscuit. And here's Father Augusto.'

Molly and I glanced at each other. She shrugged her shoulders, sat up straighter, and put on a smile.

Father Augusto appeared behind Janet, looking down at his phone.

'Father Augusto, here are the first two.'

He looked up from his phone, preparing a smile that promptly faded from his face as he recognised me. He turned to Janet, and said, 'I think there's been a mix-up. Would you mind leaving us while I sort this out? These two are not meant to be here.'

Chapter Twenty-Two

Janet, looking flustered and confused, made her way out. Father Augusto followed behind her as far as the door, then closed it, leaving the three of us alone. He returned to the sofas, but stayed standing, towering over us, arms folded in front of him, eyes narrowly glaring at us.

'Doctor Andrews. It is, to say the least, surprising to find you here. Perhaps you would like to explain?'

Before I could respond, Molly chipped in, clearly deciding that attack was the best form of defence.

'You're the one who has the explaining to do. You sniff around the museum, hungry for papyruses, and lo and behold, one goes missing. And it's about Mary Magdalene. And two days later, here you are in a shady part of town in a shady organisation called the Magdalene Initiative.'

Father Augusto put his hand on his chin, pausing while he looked at Molly. He then turned to me.

'Please, would you introduce your friend. I do not believe we have met.'

'This is Molly...' my voice tailed off as I realised I didn't know her surname. 'We are together. As in, working together.'

Smooth, I thought to myself.

'Molly Leyser,' filled in Molly.

'And you two must have followed me? Like Poirot? Hoping to find the papyrus?'

Neither of us responded. Molly kept looking at him defiantly, me a little more apologetically.

And then he began to laugh. Not a tiny gurgle, but a great roar of a laugh filling the room and drowning out the far-off noises of train engines and tracks. He kept laughing as he sat down on the other sofa, pulling a tissue from a pocket and wiping his eyes.

'I should be offended, but this is too ridiculous. And you have given me a fantastic story to tell when I get back to Rome.'

This didn't seem the type of reaction for a man who'd been caught in a cult or a brothel.

'What do you think this is?' he asked us, gesturing with his hand broadly towards the room and the building beyond.

'We're not sure, but it's quite a coincidence that it's the Magdalene Initiative,' I said.

Father Augusto leant back in the sofa, apparently completely relaxed with the situation.

'Welcome to the Magdalene Initiative. This is a Catholic charity for women who have been forced into working on the streets. We provide support for them in a whole variety of ways to help them leave that life.'

'Because Mary Magdalene was a prostitute...' said Molly, realising how badly we had judged the situation.

'And that woman we saw you with outside the alley...' I added. Father Augusto looked briefly puzzled.

'That was Lady Charlotte. She's the patron of the charity. And Mary Magdalene wasn't a prostitute either, but she certainly has been depicted as one down the ages,' said Father Augusto. 'Are you really this desperate, that you are following random priests about Manchester?'

I slumped into the sofa. 'Yes. It was a long shot, but I couldn't think of anything else useful to do.'

Molly chipped in. 'And the Vatican does have a shady history when it comes to lost gospels. And weird practices and secrets.'

Father Augusto sighed. 'People read too much nonsense. This is...' he paused, trying to find the right word, 'exciting, but not real life. In movies, murders and flagellation. In real life, meetings and conferences. And the Vatican does not go around stealing from other institutions.'

'Someone took the fragment,' I said, 'and you were showing a strong interest in it.'

'I have to admit,' he replied, 'I thought you probably took the fragment.' He looked over at me, and sighed. 'I'm sorry for your situation. I don't think I can help, but let me know if you think I can. And now, I hate to be rude, but the trustees will be arriving in a few minutes for a meeting – something about the charity being nominated for a mayor's award. I'm a special guest, invited as I'm in Manchester anyway.'

'We'd better be going, then,' I said. We all stood up, and Father Augusto showed us back to the front door.

'Sorry,' I said, as we stepped outside. He smiled, shaking his head, and waved us off.

As we left, a man and a woman, both smartly dressed, appeared at the end of the alley, peering closely at the floor to check what they might be stepping in. We briefly nodded an acknowledgement to them as we walked past, and then emerged back onto the larger road.

Molly looked at me.

I looked at Molly.

And we both started laughing uncontrollably.

Chapter Twenty-Three

'**W**hat's the plan now, Jake?' asked Molly, sipping her coffee from a speckled white porcelain mug.

We had made our way back towards Chinatown, and settled on the Manchester Art Gallery café as somewhere to sit down and regroup. I liked the tall windows flooding the large, airy space and wooden flooring with natural light. As it was still relatively early in the day, we nearly had the café to ourselves, apart from a table nearby where a group of mums were chatting, surrounded by buggies and trying to keep young toddlers amused or asleep.

I didn't answer straight away, picking up my own coffee and letting the hot, sharp aroma fill my nostrils before taking a sip. I needed time to think.

'I don't know if I have a plan any more. Mind you, I'm not sure we had much of a plan to begin with.'

'It did fall apart as soon as it encountered reality.'

'And what can we do, anyway. I mean, even if Father

Augusto had taken the fragment, how could we have proved it? He was hardly likely to confess to us.'

'I thought I did quite a mean interrogation.'

I smiled in response. I was beginning to enjoy spending time with Molly.

'I'd have liked to see you try to be mean to the American guy I met yesterday – he looked as tough as my mother's roast beef.'

'Not a great cook?'

'No. My dad did a lot of the cooking growing up. Thank goodness.'

'What about this American guy. You mentioned him last night. Could he have the papyrus?'

'Ryan. Brad Ryan.'

'He's not James Bond, is he? Ooh, is he CIA? I've always wanted to meet a spook.'

I shook my head.

'No, he works for a collector. And he wanted the papyrus. You don't offer money in a dodgy way if you already have something.'

'So we follow Brad instead of Father Augusto.'

I took another sip of coffee, then replied.

'I suppose that way we could see who he meets, and whether anyone passes him something that could be the papyrus. Bit of a long shot, though.'

'You miss a hundred percent of the chances you don't take.'

'Thank you, miss motivator. You also miss about ninety-nine point nine nine nine of the long shots you do take.'

'Well, you could try to follow Brad around with me, or you could go home and start preparing your CV.' She put her head to one side, and smiled at me.

'I hate writing CVs. Let's go the Brad route.'

'Okay, let's find out which hotel he's staying in. Bound to be one of the most expensive. Just a sec.'

Molly took out her phone, took a second to google something, then started speaking in a polite, friendly voice.

'Is that the Midland? I'm meant to be meeting Mr Brad Ryan in the foyer, but I can't remember whether he said he was staying at the Midland or the Stock Exchange.'

There was a pause while Molly listened to the answer. I continued drinking my coffee as a mother started chasing after a runaway toddler nearby.

'Oh, thank you. That's so helpful. Thanks. Bye.'

She put the phone down, and picked up her own mug, pausing to tell the news before she drank.

'The Midland it is. The game is afoot. Again.'

Chapter Twenty-Four

Our second hotel foyer of the morning, this one reeked of opulence. The floor was a light and dark brown marbled expanse, like the architect had taken inspiration from a chess board. An enormous glass roof, flooding the entire area with daylight, lit large green and purple plants that had ambitions to be trees. Molly and I had taken refuge in a couple of high-backed leather armchairs, facing at ninety degrees to each other. Between the chairs was a small, round, mahogany table, with a menu for the restaurant lying on top.

I glanced at the menu, and internally sighed. It seemed unlikely that I would soon be able to afford even a starter off the menu.

'What are you going to do if he recognises you?'

Molly's question interrupted my brief reverie of feeling sorry for myself.

'If he does, I'll pretend to be interested in his proposition. Maybe see just how much he would pay for the papyrus.'

'Are all papyruses this valuable?'

'Papyri,' I corrected.

'Oh, is it. Like octopus.'

'Well, that actually is octopuses. Or octopodes.'

Molly looked delighted at being corrected. Twice.

'Riveting,' she said.

'Sorry, no, most papyri aren't that valuable. There are loads of them floating around museums. But this one is special. It would be the oldest Christian artefact in the world, the oldest evidence of what Christianity was like, the oldest...'

'I get the picture. Special.'

The doors opened, and a couple of people entered the hotel. One of them was tall and built like a tank, holding a phone, with a white AirPod in his ear.

'That's him,' I said, gesturing in what I hoped was a discreet manner.

'Ooh, he's like a hunk of rock. Mmm.'

For some reason, Molly's positive reaction provoked a twinge of annoyance. I pushed the feeling down.

Brad Ryan marched past, talking, oblivious to our presence. We could catch a snatch of the conversation.

'...payment in parts, subject to verification. Twenty five percent tomorrow night, the rest when it's been carbon...'

He moved away to the bar area, his voice fading with his departure.

'What's that about? Has he found a seller?' asked Molly.

'Sounds that way,' I said. 'I think he was talking about carbon-dating the fragment to make sure it was genuine before stumping up all the money.'

'In that case, you can't pretend that you can negotiate with him. He's made contact with the person who has the papyrus.'

'So we can't let him see me.'

We both looked at each other, trying to work out the next move.

'Is it worth trying to get close to him in the bar?' asked Molly.

'I doubt it. He'll be off the phone in a second, and if we're too close he's going to see me. And he won't be meeting the thief until tomorrow night.'

'Well in that case, I think our work for now is done,' said Molly.

I was surprised by the pang of disappointment that leapt up at the thought of ending our time together. But Molly hadn't finished speaking.

'So, time to relax. I think you owe me lunch.'

I smiled. The day was looking up. Lunch with Molly, and a lead on the thief.

'Let's go eat. But somewhere I can afford, not here.'

Chapter Twenty-Five

'This,' said Molly, pausing while she licked some crumbs off her lips, 'is amazing.'

I smiled, and continued to tuck into my own hot ciabatta, overflowing with Italian meats, cheeses and peppers. Around us, a busy throng of customers were queuing up at the counter to order their own lunches. We had been lucky to snag a corner table. Katsouri's was a café and deli operating out of a gothic building on the corner of Deansgate and Bridge Street. Apparently, there was also one in Bury, but I had never visited.

'I come here quite often, it's close to where I work...' I came to a halt, wondering if I would ever work at the John Rylands again. I took another mouthful, hoping that it would provide cover for my pause. Molly glanced at me while continuing to bite into her ciabatta.

'Must be difficult, being suspended. Like being in limbo.'

She had noticed. I wasn't sure at first how ready I was for a conversation about my feelings on the matter.

'Why do you like your job? What is it about papyruses...' she paused, correcting herself, 'papyri? What's on them?'

'Mostly it's just everyday stuff from two thousand years ago. Letters telling their sister to buy the pigs, or bring the grain, or love spells, or accounts, or other stuff like that.'

'So not normally the lost words of Jesus. Isn't that dull?'

I paused, searching around for how to explain why I loved what I did.

'Have you heard of a photographer called Martin Parr?' I asked.

She screwed up her face, trying to remember.

'The name sounds familiar. What does he take pictures of?'

'That's the thing. He takes pictures of normal stuff. People in the supermarket, or shopping, or in their homes. Filling up the car at the petrol station. Ordinary stuff.'

Molly looked confused. 'But that sounds dull.'

'They had an exhibition of his stuff at Manchester Art Gallery a while back. But the thing about the photos, is that he took the pictures back in the seventies, and it was like entering a time machine. The photos transported you to a different world. And that's why people love his stuff. What's ordinary now becomes extraordinary when time passes.'

'And it's the same with the papyri?'

'You've got it. They open up this lost world. Their everyday concerns, loves, quarrels and records are like a torchlight on the dark past.'

Molly laughed, but sympathetically.

'Alright, no need to get poetic. But I can see why you might like what you do. And I'm sorry it's been affected.'

I decided to open up.

'It's horrible. This is my whole professional career, my

academic career, going up in smoke. And I have no control over it. I mean, we're running around after these people, but what difference will it make? If they did take it, they're hardly likely to tell me about it.'

I paused, and Molly let the silence rest between us. Then I carried on.

'I'm angry now. At first, I was just bewildered, and kept on thinking, this can't be happening to me. But now I'm riled. My life is being destroyed, and someone else is to blame.'

I had surprised myself. Until I spoke the words, I hadn't realised how furious I had become. It had been masked by having a good morning with Molly, but now the feeling was flooding over me.

'So what next?'

I didn't answer at first. I was trying to work out in my own mind what to do. But there weren't any good answers.

'I don't know. In two days, I'm likely to be sacked from my position by the board. And I've got nothing except a few frail threads to grasp onto. The only lead is hoping that we see who Brad Ryan meets tomorrow night.'

Molly squished up her face, thinking. 'It's not the only lead. There's also that group of vicars who came on the visit. What do we know about them?'

I thought back. 'I don't know. They seemed to know each other quite well, but only the woman was really interested in what I was doing. The other two seemed a bit bored.'

'Could we find out who she is?'

I looked doubtful. 'I guess so. I could ask Pete.'

'And Pete is...'

'One of the guards at the John Rylands. He might know who the group were, or have a record of them. They might have had to sign in or something.'

Molly turned and faced me directly.

'Do you want to keep doing this? You've said yourself it's a thin thread, and it might just be another waste of your time. Would you rather do something else? I can clear off if you'd rather just go somewhere and try and process what's been happening to you.'

The thought of Molly clearing off did not bring joy to me. And now I realised I was angry, I needed to do something, anything, to try to clear my name.

'If you're still up for it, I'm in. Let's go and find out who those priests were.'

Molly laughed. 'At least let me finish my ciabatta.'

Chapter Twenty-Six

'You're lucky I'm in a good mood. I'll check the system.' Pete, a security guard at the John Rylands, moved to a small computer at a desk, and started tapping out a password. 'You're up to your neck in it, aren't you?'

'Yep, so thanks – I need all the help I can get.'

He continued tapping away, occasionally moving the mouse to the right of the keyboard. 'Hey, I bought the paper with your face on. Could I get you to autograph it? Little bit of history there.'

This was a request I had not expected.

'Really?'

'Yes.' He looked around at me and grinned. 'When you're cleared, it'll be a nice souvenir of a big event at the John Rylands.' He paused, before continuing, 'And if you're guilty, it'll be worth even more.'

'Thanks. Thanks a bunch. You really know how to make someone feel better.'

Pete laughed. 'I'll visit you in prison. Send a file in a cake or something. And will you be waiting for him?' This last comment was directed to Molly.

I blushed, and then blushed some more as I realised I was blushing, and was hoping that Molly wasn't noticing that I was blushing.

'Are you blushing?' asked Peter, back to me.

'We aren't a... she isn't my...'

Molly put me out of my misery.

'We're friends. And I don't like prisons, so he's on his own if he's guilty.'

Pete turned back to the screen. 'Anyway,' he said to Molly as he scanned the documents flashing up, 'you can do better. Much better.'

I kept quiet. There didn't seem a response I could make which wouldn't make me blush more.

'Here we go. Monday's visit. Five visitors booked in for a tour with Professor Richard Chelworth. Mr Brad Ryan, Antiquities Consultant. Father Augusto Zappacosta, the Vatican. Reverend Matthew Ascough, parish of St Ursula, Reverend Geraldine Sutcliffe, parish of St Hildegard, and Reverend Guy Ross-Lindon, parish of St Elfin. That's your lot.'

'Thanks Pete, you're a star; I owe you one.'

'Then sign this,' he said, handing over a copy of the Mirror and a ballpoint pen. He had it open on a crossword, partially completed. Molly peered over.

'Oh, I love crosswords. I used to do them with my aunt. Can I have a look?'

Pete's face took on a pained expression; clearly, he didn't want anyone else to finish off his crossword, but was struggling to say so politely. I flipped over the pages back to the front page, hoping to head off an awkward moment.

'Here I am. I'll sign it under the photo,' I said, scrawling on the paper before handing it back to him with the pen.

'That's one for the scrapbook. Now clear off before anyone important comes in.'

He put the paper and pen down, logged off the computer, straightened up, and smiled.

'Good luck. You'll need it.'

As we moved outside, Molly called back, '19 across – it's macaroni. Tubular pasta, eight letters.' She smiled. Pete's face returned to its slightly pained version, and we exited onto a large, sunlit pedestrianised space. A skateboarder with ripped jeans and vintage style t-shirt was making use of the wide expanse to practise some tricks. He needed the practice. Molly glanced over at him, then turned her face back to me.

'Three vicars. Which do we go far?'

I thought back for a minute. 'The two male clergy looked as though they thought they ought to be interested, but weren't really. You know, like people who pretend they like opera but would really rather be watching a soap.'

'Okay,' said Molly, 'that leaves Geraldine of Hildenburg.'

'Hildegard,' I corrected automatically. And then blushed, in case she thought I was mansplaining. But Molly appeared oblivious, typing into her phone.

'Here we go. It's Hildegard, not Hildenburg. Who was Hildegard? Anyway, the church is only a five-minute walk away, according to Google Maps. Is it the main church for the city? I'd have thought that was the Cathedral.'

'No, the city centre church is St. Ann's. I hadn't heard of St Hildegard's church before.'

Molly briefly looked up and around, then down to the phone screen, then up again.

'This way.' And she strode off towards Deansgate. I

followed after, catching her up at the traffic lights. She was peering at her phone again.

'It's peculier.'

'The whole thing is a bit strange,' I responded.

'No, well yes, but no. I meant the church. It's a royal peculier church. The king, not the local bishop, gets to control it.'

The lights changed, the cars reluctantly halted, and we crossed over, and then carried straight on down a pedestrianised side road. Modern, dark red brick buildings towered either side, looking ideal for city centre law firms and marketing agencies. A handful of bikes were locked to metallic rails in the centre of the road. Molly then took a left past some steel bollards onto a smaller, brick-covered side road that bent around a corner. There was nothing obviously there beyond on the left a courtyard of a diner, with aluminium chairs and tables, and more offices on the right.

'I've read some more. Apparently, Hildegard was some old abbess from the Middle Ages. Told kings off and wrote music and poetry.'

'You can still buy her music. There's an album of her stuff.'

Molly turned down the sides of her mouth and wrinkled her nose. 'You're kidding me.'

'No, some choral group recorded her music. *A Feather On The Breath Of God*. She won album of the year in the eighties.'

Molly raised an eyebrow, and returned to her phone. Then raised her other eyebrow. 'She really did. Way to go, girl.'

The street did not look promising. We walked past a row of industrial rubbish bins, some grey and others blue and orange. The buildings began to seem less suitable for professionals.

'Are you sure this is right?' I asked, as we passed a couple of steel garage doors for underground car parks.

And then, in between red brick offices, I saw the church. It was hidden at first, built out of the same bricks. But as you drew closer, more details became obvious. The front had arched windows, and looking up revealed a large round window below a tower. Three stone steps led up to oversize, dark oak doors broken up with stained glass panels. The left-hand door stood slightly ajar. To the right, a black notice board in white gothic lettering announced the church of St. Hildegard, and gave the times of services.

'Yes, I'm sure this is right. Let's go in and meet Geraldine.'

Without waiting, Molly pushed open the left-hand door, and ventured in. As the door opened wider, low chants drifted out, a medley of voices murmuring. I followed after Molly towards the sound, leaving the brightness of the world outside for the gloom inside the church.

Chapter Twenty-Seven

'It's some sort of service going on,' Molly whispered.

We had emerged from a gloomy porch through another set of doors into a vast, bright expanse. Dark oak rafters stood out against the whitewashed walls and ceilings. Marble pillars formed a guard of honour for long wooden pews flanking a red-carpeted central aisle. The smell of polish mixed with a faint aroma of incense. At the end of the aisle, two steps led up to a large chancel area. Behind a stone slab of an altar table, a priest in white robes and a green scarf held her arms out wide, as she prayed in a sing-song chant. I peered closer. It was the female minister who had visited the John Rylands: Geraldine Sutcliffe.

'Jesus is the Lamb of God who takes away the sin of the world. Blessed are those who are called to his supper.'

The congregation murmured a response, 'Lord, I am not worthy to receive you, but only say the word, and I shall be healed.'

We crept into the last pew on the right-hand side.

'What's going on?' whispered Molly.

'Communion. Also called Mass.'

My voice was masked by shuffling, as people started moving from their pews into an orderly central queue. The priest moved in front of the altar to the top of the steps leading into the chancel. A man who looked as if he might have middle eastern heritage stood by her side, holding the silver chalice. At the front of the queue, worshippers bowed their heads and stretched out their hands together to receive a wafer from the priest, then shifted sideways to take a sip from the silver chalice.

'I remember now, we did this in RS at school. I've never been to one before. No-one in my family goes to church,' said Molly.

An elderly lady at the end of the queue, hair bleached white over many decades, looked over in our direction and smiled. She raised her eyebrows and nodded towards the front, inviting us to join. I mouthed 'thank you' and put up a hand indicating that we would stay seated.

Molly seemed fascinated, as though she were a nine-teenth century anthropologist discovering weird rituals.

'Is this... normal?'

'Yes. Bog standard communion service in the Church of England. Slightly on the high side, I'm guessing, as they sometimes use incense. But definitely normal.'

The worshippers began to return to their pews. Once the queue had finished, the priest returned to behind the altar, and cleaned out the chalice and paten.

'Is she doing the washing up? Do men priests have to do that?'

'It's more symbolic washing up, and yes, it's nothing to do with gender.'

Molly continued staring around, eyes wide with delight,

as everyone launched into saying a prayer together. When everyone else then stood, Molly joined in. I followed suit, just in time for the priest to pronounce a blessing on everyone, making a large cross sign with her arm. A final prayer, and everyone sat down again, bowed their heads, and then began getting up and chatting with those near them.

'Would you like a coffee? It's not very good, but we do have biscuits. At least, we should do.'

The elderly lady smiled again with this invitation, and carried on talking to us.

'It's just through that door over there,' she pointed towards the side aisle on our right, '...and then up the stairs to the meeting room.'

Molly and I exchanged glances, I shrugged my shoulders, and we turned back to the woman.

'Thank you, that would be lovely. And would we be able to speak to the minister?'

'Oh, I hope so. Normally Mother Geraldine manages to stay for a coffee and a quick chat.'

We thanked the lady again, and made our way to the side door.

'*Mother* Geraldine?'

'Yes. Again, pretty normal if you're from the more Anglo-Catholic side of the Church of England.'

The other side of the door was a wooden, spiral staircase that led up to a large room, with magnolia walls, wooden floors and a stage at one end, currently curtained off. At the opposite end, another door opened up into a kitchen, with a hatch cut through back to the main space. A couple of cream-coloured long tables, the type that fold up for storage, sat strategically near the hatch, with chairs scattered round them. Columns of stacked chairs lined parts of the walls. About half the congregation had made it up, some gathered in small groups round the tables, others standing and chatting, and some queuing patiently at the hatch.

The man who had been assisting the minister noticed our entrance, and approached us, a smile on his face.

'Hi, welcome to Hildie's. I'm Hasan. Can I get you a tea or coffee?'

We ended up sitting on a table with Maureen, the elderly lady who had directed us up the stairs, and Hasan, who told us how he had come originally from Iran, but now had indefinite leave to remain in Britain. Maureen had been right about the coffee. It was awful, managing a weird combination of being both too weak and also slightly bitter.

As I was contemplating how such a brew could be made, Mother Geraldine burst through the door. She was no longer in white robes, but wearing, like she had when visiting the John Rylands, a black clerical shirt with white dog collar and black trousers.

'Tea please, Margaret,' she called out to the kitchen, before glancing around the room. On seeing our table, she looked again, more attentively, and lifted one eyebrow. Then she strode to the hatch, picked up the cup now awaiting her ('thanks, Margaret') and resumed striding to our table, where she sat down next to Hasan and Maureen, and opposite Molly and me.

'I do believe we have a celebrity in our midst. Doctor Andrews, welcome to St Hildegard's. And this is...?' She turned her face towards Molly.

'Molly. Not a doctor.'

'Well, Molly not a doctor, hello.' She turned her attention back to me.

'Doctor Andrews, I was not expecting to see you. May I be blunt? Why are you here?'

The forthright questioning took me by surprise, and I began to respond by floundering and stuttering. Molly stepped in.

'We're hunting the missing papyrus fragment. And you were one of the last people present before it disappeared.'

Geraldine leant back in her chair, folding her arms.

'You're looking for the missing papyrus?'

'Yes,' said Molly, firmly.

Geraldine frowned slightly. 'And are you connected with the official police investigation?'

'No, but we think they're just blaming Jake rather than finding the real suspect.'

'You do know that I have been interviewed by the police?'

We did not know that.

'And you do know that so have my colleagues who I dragged along on that day? They did not appreciate the experience.'

We did not know that either.

'And you expect, as the chief suspect and,' Geraldine paused, and looked again at Molly, 'whoever you are, to turn up here, and find the papyrus.'

'We were following a lead,' I said, realising as I was speaking that it sounded lame.

'And what was your cunning plan? That I am a skilled relics thief, able to shift the blame to you, and to brush off police interviews, but if you asked me over coffee I would crumble and confess to everything? Was that really your plan, or have I missed something?'

I had not expected a priest to be quite so sarcastic.

'I had nothing better to do,' I said, defensively. 'The country thinks I'm a thief, my employer is about to sack me, and the police are looking to arrest me. I don't have many good options.'

'And this certainly wasn't a good option.' Geraldine then sighed, and unfolded her arms to reach a small black note-book and Bic pen.

I said, 'By the way, you shouldn't use a ballpoint pen in the John Rylands. We try to avoid anything that might accidentally permanently mark one of the collection. Pencils only.'

Geraldine lifted her eyes to mine, held them for a second to check that I was serious, shook her head a little and returned her gaze to her notebook.

'You seem desperate, so I'll tell you what I told the police. Really desperate.' She flicked through the pages.

'Here we are. Monday. A visit to the John Rylands Library, as part of a private tour. It got advertised in the diocesan mailing, but only I was interested. I persuaded Matty – that's Matthew Ascough – and Guy Ross-Lindon to come along. They were both bored throughout. I'd be amazed if either of them was interested enough to nick a biro, let alone a papyrus, but in any case they wouldn't. Then there was the Vatican man, Augusto something. He seemed to know his stuff. And a tall American. Brad Ryan. He was one of the last to leave your room. Of the group, it was Matty and Guy first, then me, then Augusto and Brad. If it was one of us visitors, I'd put my money on him.'

'We thought that too, but we think he's buying it off someone tomorrow night. We overheard a bit of a conversation.'

'And what did the police make of this information?'

A long, uncomfortable silence followed. I found myself looking carefully at my shoes.

'I mean, you did tell the police? Because only absolute idiots would think they could do it themselves. Only absolute idiots would make a plan to see if they could catch Mister Ryan with the papyrus when they could just tell the police. Only absolute idiots would...'

'Alright, we're idiots,' I interrupted.

'Absolute idiots,' said Geraldine, emphasising absolute. 'If you both thought this was a good idea, you deserve each other.'

'You've made your point,' said Molly. 'We'll contact the police. But what if they don't listen to us? It's easy to leave it to someone else when it's not your career on the line.'

'You don't have the authority, the training, the equipment or the human resources for intercepting someone receiving stolen goods. Please, for your own sakes, leave it to the professionals.'

Hasan joined in.

'You could tell the police, but still follow him at a distance. If you see police around, pull out. If you don't, try to get a photo when he meets the other person.'

'Oh, yes,' said Maureen. 'It sounds exciting. I could do with some excitement myself. You go for it. You're only young once, and you always regret the things you didn't do more than the things you did.' And she sighed, and looked into space for a moment. 'Alf Greenhalgh. I regret not doing him...'

I blushed. Molly smirked. Hasan looked a little shocked, and Geraldine rolled her eyes, as though she was used to this from Maureen.

Geraldine retook control.

'In any case, you must first tell the police.'

Molly and I looked at each other, and both of us nodded. I replied, 'Okay, as soon as I'm...' I paused briefly as I realised that the contact details for DS Penry were lying on my kitchen work top, '...as soon as I'm back at my home I'll give the detective a ring. That's where I've got her contact details.'

'Yes,' said Molly, emphatically. 'We'll do it as soon as we have the details.'

The visit to the church had not exactly been a triumph, but I felt strangely cheered by the prospect of spending a bit more time with Molly.

Chapter Twenty-Eight

The bus ride home was another opportunity to chat with Molly. We sat upstairs at the front as the yellow double decker bus jolted and jerked its way down Oxford Road, the rumble of the engine interspersed with the hissing as the doors below opened and closed at each stop. The red brick buildings we passed glowed in the sunshine against a deep blue sky. It would have been delightful, except for a stale smell of chicken takeaway that seemed to infuse this particular bus. I pointed out some of the landmarks.

'That's Manchester Aquatics, great for serious swimmers. They built it for the Commonwealth Games. Bit cold for my liking. And that on our right is the Manchester Museum.'

I pointed to a honey-coloured building with arches, turrets and towers that stretched on for what must have been over a hundred yards. It gave off mellow gothic overtones.

'They've refurbished it recently, and it has a nice vegetarian café attached. And the rest of this is all the University of Manchester. And on the left, that large tin can is also a university building.'

I pointed at a stainless-steel curved building on our left, that looked like a gigantic tin can, the sun's rays blinding as they bounced off it.

'What's its name?'

'I don't know, but everyone calls it the tin can. There are lecture theatres inside.'

I wasn't convinced that I was doing well as a tour guide, and fell silent for a couple of minutes. But then Molly piped up.

'What's this collection of buildings, all different styles?' Molly asked, gesturing to our left.

'It's hospitals. More than one. Let's see, the Eye Hospital, the MRI–'

'MRI?'

'The Manchester Royal Infirmary. It's a general hospital, you know, A&E and surgery and everything. And there's also the Children's Hospital, and St Mary's, which is babies and stuff.'

'Babies and stuff.'

I could feel my cheeks flushing a little. 'Women and babies and pregnancy stuff.'

'I think I can tell you're not a doctor of medicine. It's big. And what's that?'

Molly pointed to the other side of the road at a large, red-brick, two-storey building with a semi-circular entrance adorned with classical looking pillars.

'That's the Whitworth Art Gallery. It has a nice café. And textiles and stuff.'

Molly snorted. 'Are there any museum cafés you haven't tried?'

I smiled and shook my head. The bus rumbled on into a stretch of Asian and middle eastern restaurants and shops.

'This is the Curry Mile – look, it's even got banners telling you it's the famous Curry Mile. Except it's not a mile long, and lots of the food is not curries.'

Molly's eyes darted from colourful shopfront to shopfront, fascinated by the variety. Every other storefront was a restaurant or café, with signs in bright, primary colours. The shops interspersed offered sumptuous clothes for special occasions, Asian sweets, jewellery and an unusually high number of barbers, all with interiors gleaming with stainless steel and promising precise shaves.

'I bet this is fantastic at night. I love Asian food,' she said. 'You're so lucky living this close. I suppose you're here all the time.'

I confessed that I spent more time eating at a little Greek takeaway in Fallowfield that was furnished with a few tables where you could sit down to consume your food. Molly shook her head, implying I was wasting a golden opportunity.

'I bet you always choose kormas. Chicken korma. And a plain naan. Tell me I'm wrong.'

I grinned. 'You're not wrong.'

A smile flickered on her face, and then she turned towards me, a more serious look in her eye.

'I'm sorry today's been a washout. I can't imagine what this is like for you. And thank you for showing me around Manchester – it's been a great way to get to know some of the city.'

I shrugged my shoulders, and tried to look stoical.

'It is what it is. And I'm glad you got something out of the day.'

'And maybe the police will be able to do something about

that American buying the fragment. Things still might work out.'

The comment triggered other thoughts in my head, about trying to work things out. I pulled out my phone and began texting.

'I'm going to ask Professor Chelworth for an informal meeting tomorrow morning, off John Rylands ground. At the very least maybe I can get him to persuade the board to postpone any decisions until the police enquiry is finished.'

I pressed send, and leaned back in my seat. The bus had made its way through the curry mile, and now emerged into a more open area, with a large park to the right: Platt Fields.

'It's nearly our stop. We'd better get downstairs.'

We made our way down, as the bus jostled along the road, grabbing onto the yellow handrails to make sure we didn't slip as we descended. Half way down, my phone beeped. Once I had reached the bottom, I fished it out. Professor Chelworth had said yes to a meeting. Thursday ten o'clock at Caffè Nero on Deansgate. I felt a small surge of hope well up inside. With a combination of a suspect to offer the police, and a chance to make my case to the professor, if I squinted I could see a silver lining.

The bus pulled to a halt, and breathed a sigh as the floor lowered and the doors pulled apart. I said thanks to the driver, and Molly and I got off, along with a woman carrying a small dog. The bus sighed again, the doors closed, and it pulled away.

'I'm on the other side of the road,' I said, and we waited for a gap in the traffic before crossing over, and making our way down the side road towards my house.

'I need to get something from the corner shop,' said Molly.

'Anything in particular? I might have it in the house.'

Molly's face flushed slightly. 'With two men in the house I doubt it. Give me your house number, and I'll be along in a minute.'

I gave her the number, and she turned off towards the corner shop. I walked up to the front door, glad to see that the lock had remained intact.

Next step, I thought, as I reached for my key, would be to phone the police. Then I felt a heavy thud on the back of my neck, and everything went dark.

Chapter Twenty-Nine

A bowling ball in a shopping trolley careered erratically inside my head, bouncing repeatedly off the skull. I had experienced headaches before, but those had been like mild taps compared with the vicious assault currently taking place. I gingerly went to feel my neck for any damage, only to find my hands wouldn't move, but were stuck by the side of my legs. A constant thudding completed the attack. Fighting back waves of pain and nausea, I cracked open my eyes.

Dark grey kitchen units. I was sat in a chair in my kitchen. I shifted my head a little, and regretted it.

'He's back. Time for a nice chat. Spud, put on the kettle.'

The voice came from my right. I looked around. A man with neat, straight dark hair parted to the side and with blue eyes stared back. He looked to be mid-thirties, but trying hard to stay young-looking. He wore a charcoal grey suit with a thin red stripe, with a pale pink open-necked shirt, which clashed with his fake-tanned skin. A thick golden watch with a gold chain-link strap adorned his left wrist. His black shoes looked expensive, and looked like they wanted you to know they were expensive.

From behind me, someone tall brushed past and flicked the kettle on.

I slowly became aware that the thudding sound wasn't just in my head, but that Mr B was not taking the situation well, and was thumping his disapproval.

I tried to speak, and realised that not only were my hands zip-tied to the base of the chair, but that there was tape covering my mouth.

I took a deep breath through my nose, and tried not to be sick. I didn't like to think of the consequences given my taped mouth.

The man named Spud was about six foot four, wearing a crisp white t-shirt above dark blue Levi 501 jeans. He had a long, rectangular face with grey eyes and short, blond hair combed into a fringe on his forehead. He had a wiry build, the sort I associated with climbers. He started humming tunelessly to himself, as he first pressed the button on the kettle, and then started opening cupboards randomly.

'Mmm mmm mmm,' I tried.

'Take the tape off, Axel. Time for talkies.'

From behind me, another person (presumably Axel) reached over me to the right side of my face, grabbed the tape, and yanked hard. I momentarily saw tiny sparks floating around my eyes, which was little compensation for the jolt of pain that shot through my mouth area, as a thousand nerve endings screamed in unison.

'Ow. Ow. Ow. Ow. Ow.' It wasn't my most imaginative response to the situation, but on the other hand it did fit the circumstances quite well.

Mr B thumped again. The kettle started to build up a head of steam, literally.

'So, now it's time to help us,' said the man in the suit, or suit-man as I decided to name him until further information emerged.

'They're in the drawer. We keep them in the drawer, middle unit, right hand side. My right.'

Suit-man raised his right eyebrow. 'That was quick.'

Spud opened the drawer in question. 'Ah,' he said, 'mugs.' He looked at his boss and shrugged. Mr B thumped again.

Suit-man leaned closer in towards my right ear. 'Are you trying to make me angrier? Because you're doing a fantastic job of it.' Another thump from Mr B. 'And will someone sort out that rabbit? It's doing my head in.'

Axel, from behind me, piped up. 'It's just anxious. Probably not used to this many people in the kitchen. Natural response of rabbits. Bet they're a cutie normally, aren't they?'

Surprised to be asked this, I hesitantly responded, 'Er, not really. He's quite a bad-tempered rabbit, if I'm honest.'

'Is he on his own? Tell me you have another rabbit. Do you?'

The interrogation had taken a turn I hadn't really counted on. 'No, just Mr B, he's on his own here.'

Axel came around in front of me. Someone had clearly taken a barrelful of muscles and dumped them into his frame. And then added an extra couple of barrels just for luck. Biceps bulged out of a faded black t-shirt. Jeans looked in danger of bursting from thighs each thick as Nelson's Column. He didn't seem to possess much of a neck; a square-jawed, close-shaven head topped the barrels. And right now, with eyebrows furrowed, a mean glint in his dark brown eyes, and clenched fists, just like Mr B he did not look like a happy bunny.

'Rabbits are social animals,' he growled, 'used to living in warrens as part of a large group. They are not meant to be solo. No wonder he's bad tempered.' Then he stepped over to the hutch, undid the two plastic clips holding the wire side to the base, and lifted up the side. He knelt down, and scooped up Mr B in two hands, before holding him in his arms.

I inwardly winced (easy as I needed to wince anyway from the headache), ready for Mr B to kick, bite or scratch him. But it didn't happen. At first Mr B's ears went flat on the back of his head, but then they relaxed back to their more usual position hanging vertically, as Axel sat on one of the other kitchen chairs and placed the rabbit on his knees, stroking him from head to tail.

'Does he normally get the run of the house?'

'No, he stays in his cage–'

I was interrupted by Axel's sharp intake of breath. I had thought he was glaring before, but it turned out that had been merely a disapproving glance compared with the ferocity of his current stare.

'Do you know nothing about rabbits? Or just not care?'

I confessed my ignorance. Axel began shaking his head, and muttering darkly under his breath.

The man in the suit took over again. 'Ah, the kettle's boiling. We're ready.'

'Teabags are in the tin on the counter, and there's a bag of sugar somewhere in the cupboard on the left. And the milk in the fridge should still be okay, it's only a day or two past the sell-by.' I decided to be as helpful as possible, in the hope that it might mollify my attackers.

'Bless. He thinks we boiled the kettle for a cup of tea,' the man said to Axel and Spud. Then he turned his head back to me, and with great deliberation said, 'The boiling water is for you, if you don't tell us everything.'

And then the doorbell rang, and Molly shouted out from the hallway, 'Hi, I'm back.'

Chapter Thirty

The man in the suit looked at Axel and raised his right eyebrow. Axel looked at Spud, and said, 'I thought you locked the front door?'

Spud shrugged his shoulders, and said, 'I thought you did.'

And by the time they had had this exchange, Molly was opening the kitchen door.

Spud moved with surprising speed and grace, and grabbed Molly by the arm and pulled her inside the kitchen before she had even had time for a shocked expression to register on her face. Meanwhile, suit-man had hooked another kitchen chair with his foot, and slid it towards Spud, who promptly pushed Molly down to sit on it. By now Molly was gathering breath ready for a yell, but Axel, in one fluid movement, had placed Mr B gently on the floor, come from behind her and now covered her mouth with his right hand, holding onto her left arm with his free hand. Suit-man fished a couple of cable ties from his right pocket, passing them to Spud, who fastened her right hand to the chair, followed in smooth succession by her left. Finally, Spud picked up the reel of tape, ripped off a bit, and with Axel's help covered her mouth. The whole process took under three seconds.

It was awful to watch, but also deeply impressive, like seeing a Formula One race team perform a pit stop. I decided that, assuming we got through this, I would refrain from telling Molly this.

'Well,' said suit-man, 'this changes things. This is your girlfriend?'

'No, well, we only met recently...' My voice trailed off, as I tried to work out the safest answer to the question. My eyes locked with Molly's, whose eyes were showing a mixture of shock, fear and anger. Meanwhile, Spud was emptying the pockets of her suit.

'Molly C. Leyser,' he announced, peering at a credit card. He took out his phone, and typed one-handed. 'Here we go, active on Instagram. Oh, she's got a cousin here as well. Maisy Roberts.'

I didn't like where this investigation was going.

On hearing the name, suit-man paused, peered at Molly, and then shook his head briefly. 'Right, back to business,' he said. 'Why has that kettle not stopped boiling, Spud?' Spud promptly turned off the kettle. I made a mental note to splash out on a new one should I survive this experience.

'Please, not the kettle.'

'What?' He seemed surprised, as he turned to me. 'Oh, sorry, that was just my joke. We do want some cups of tea.'

My whole body relaxed a little.

'No, we're going to use these,' Spud said, reaching to the floor and pulling a pair of short-handled garden loppers out of a black rucksack. They oozed sturdiness, as though there was no tree branch in the world that would stand against them.

'Like *Line of Duty*,' said Axel, 'only ours work.'

'I haven't seen it yet,' I replied.

'Oh, then sorry for any plot spoilers. But it's worth catching. BBC iPlayer. Cracking show.'

'So,' said Spud, 'let me explain how this is going to work. We are going to ask you questions. And if we aren't happy with an answer, she loses a finger. Understand?'

You know how at the dentist they have a little sucky vacuum thing that removes all the water from your mouth? It felt like someone had used an industrial version on me. Or emptied one of those desiccating packets into the insides of my mouth. Meanwhile, Spud, Axel and suit-man seemed calm and relaxed, as if what was going on was the most normal event in the world. Their equanimity was, if anything, even more ominous than if they had been furious.

'She's got nothing to do with this. She was just popping by. I only met her yesterday. You don't need to involve her–' My burbling was interrupted by Spud.

'First question. And, hopefully, the last. Nice and simple.' He paused, and Axel interrupted him.

'Hold on. First things first. Where's the tea?'

Spud laughed. 'I forgot I was making them. Hold on a bit.' He turned back to the kitchen units, and started whistling tunelessly as he re-boiled the kettle, turned it off manually when it began spitting steam again, added teabags to three mugs, and found the sugar and teaspoons.

'It's criminal how you're treating that rabbit. That cage is too small for him to live in, you don't let him out, and he's on his own.' Axel was still unhappy with the treatment of Mr B.

'Do you have rabbits?' I asked. It seemed a safer topic than anything involving the amputation of fingers.

'Four. All adopted from the RSPCA. We converted one of our rooms.'

'Do you have young children?' In my mind, people usually got rabbits as pets for this reason, with Pete being an outlier. But Axel looked offended.

'Rabbits aren't a pet for young children,' he scoffed. 'You know nothing.' And a scowl settled like a dark cloud on his face again.

'Tea's ready,' said Spud, and passed a mug to Axel and suit-man. I decided not to protest that Molly and I were not included. Axel blew on it, took a sip, and the cloud took on a lighter tone. Spud also took a sip of his mug, then placed it back on the kitchen unit.

'Now, where were we?' He leaned down, and picked up the loppers, opening and closing them a couple of times to ensure they worked. Molly began straining in her chair, pulling against the ties, which held firm.

'Hold on,' said Axel, 'Where did the rabbit go?'

Chapter Thirty-One

We all looked round, even Molly, who to be fair could have had other things on her mind. Like if she would ever play the piano again. If she did play the piano. I didn't know much about her yet. It would be nice to get the opportunity. With all her fingers still intact.

'You did close the front door this time?' Axel asked Spud. Spud shook his head. 'Too busy getting Molly C. Leyser safely tied up.'

Axel muttered under his breath, and marched out of the room. As he went, he commanded Spud, 'check the upstairs. I'm going to look outside and check the downstairs.'

'Didn't know rabbits could climb stairs,' said Spud. But he went out of the kitchen to check.

'Well, this is upsetting,' said suit-man. While I was glad that he showed such concern for animals, and no doubt occasionally donated to the RSPCA, I couldn't help but notice that he seemed less concerned by how many fingers Molly or I ended up with by the time they had finished.

He pushed himself up from his chair, and gave a perfunctory peer round the room.

'He hasn't gone back into his cage, has he? The covered bit?' I asked. And then wondered why I was trying to shorten the time until the threatened torture began. Suit-man crouched down and peered into the cage.

'Nah, not here. I'm more of a dog man myself.' Suit-man then straightened up.

I decided to try to make conversation. I had a vague memory that you should try to humanise yourself with captors, to make it harder for them psychologically to hurt you.

'Do you prefer dogs because they care more about their owners? You know, like cats ignore you, rabbits acknowledge you, and dogs adore you?'

'That, and because it's difficult to train a rabbit to take a chunk out of someone's leg or arm.'

This wasn't the encouraging answer I was hoping for, but I ploughed on. 'I expect your kids love having dogs around, too.'

'You kidding? I wouldn't let my Megan anywhere near my dogs. They'd rip her to shreds.' He paused, and then carried on. 'Well, they might not, but I'd rather not take the risk.'

'And how old is Megan?'

'Megs? She's seventeen. Learning to drive, would you believe it. All I can say is, driving instructors earn every penny.' And he shook his head, as though recalling a time when he had faced the gates of hell themselves.

'You don't look old enough to have a daughter that age,' I said. This was a mixture of an attempt to curry favour, and also I was genuinely surprised. His face was free of lines, and I had guessed his age as being about mid-thirties.

'I married my childhood sweetheart. Started going out together at sixteen. Still together now,' he said, looking pleased.

'That's lovely,' I said. 'While we're waiting, can I check how you like being addressed?'

He laughed. 'You asking me what my name is?'

'Well, yes, but I don't want to be forward.'

'You can call me Mr Bloodsmith. Craig to my friends. Tell you what, just call me Craig.'

He seemed cheerily unconcerned giving me these details about himself. It wasn't reassuring, although there was the faint inference that I might be considered a friend.

A voice came from upstairs, 'it's here. It's gone under a bed.'

The next sound was the front door shutting, and then a clomp of feet as Axel made his way up the stairs.

'Well, that's okay then. We can get back to where we were.' Craig then turned towards the hallway, and shouted, 'Come on then, I'm waiting.'

Muffled sounds of a heated conversation filtered downstairs. Then Spud appeared, brow furrowed.

'Axel says we can't leave the rabbit there. And,' he turned his head to me at this point, 'do you have any salad? Like coriander or something?'

'I think there's some greens in the bottom of the fridge. In the salad compartment.'

Spud crouched down, opened the fridge door, and took out the greens. He tore off a handful, shut the fridge door, and rushed back upstairs.

'Sorry about Axel,' Craig said, 'he's a bit soft when it comes to animals.'

'Nobody's perfect,' I said.

'*Some Like It Hot*, am I right? That was a funny film. Love Jack Lemmon.'

'It is good, but I think *the Apartment* is better. Greater range of emotions.'

'That's fighting talk. But I'll grant you *the Apartment* is pure class.'

'Anything by Wilder is class. Like *the Front Page*.'

Craig chuckled to himself at this. 'It's good, but *His Girl Friday* is better.'

'Never seen it.' I was hopeful that bonding over classic films would help when Mr B was tempted out from under the bed. Meanwhile, Molly was rolling her eyes. I wasn't sure whether it was over the film choice or making friends with a putative torturer.

'Oh, you've got a treat. Fastest talking in a movie, ever. Howard Hughes made sure of that. And Cary Grant being Cary Grant. Did you know it was first a stage–'

'Got 'im!' Axel shouted from upstairs. And a few seconds later, Spud came back into the kitchen, followed by Axel triumphantly carrying Mr B, who was busy munching his way through some greens.

'Order is restored. All is well with the world. Now, put the bunny back in the cage, and maybe we can get home so I can spend some quality time with my wife and daughter.'

Axel nodded at Craig, then scowled at me. 'You had better sort this out. It's not right,' he said, carefully replacing Mr B into his red cage, and fastening the plastic flaps.

Craig checked that the rabbit was safe and secure, and that Axel and Spud were both free of any distractions.

'Gentlemen,' he said to them both, 'let's get to work.'

Spud reached down, and picked up the loppers again. In the other chair, Molly's eyes widened.

'So, what's your answer?' asked Spud.

I paused a second. 'I don't think you've asked me a question yet.' I tried desperately to sound helpful and not sarcastic. 'What would you like to know?'

There was a second's silence.

It is surprising just how long a second can last, in certain contexts. Mostly, they fly by, swiftly followed by another. But this second hung around, making its presence felt. It created room for pictures of the future (mostly grim, involving blood and severed fingers) as its stillness touched everything in the kitchen.

And then Craig guffawed.

'He's right. We never asked him a question. Spud, have you got a question for him?'

'Why don't birds fall out of trees when they're asleep?'

Craig nodded approvingly. 'Good question. Your turn, Axel.'

'To what extent is Homer a fictional character as much as any of the characters in the Iliad itself?'

Craig put his head to one side. 'Really, Axel? That's your question?'

'He has got a point,' I said. 'Modern scholarship often sees Homer as more of a composite character created through many years of combining oral compositions...'

I trailed off, as Craig was now staring at me much as a cat might stare at a mouse that decided to do a stand-up routine by the cat's food bowl.

'Funnily enough, smart guy, those are not the questions I seek an answer to today.' The guffaw was long gone. Craig was now emanating an icy menace, with each word carefully enunciated to ensure complete clarity of understanding.

'My question is this. Where is it?'

I gulped, and then gave them the answer that I hoped would lead to Molly and I being freed.

'My name is Jake.'

Chapter Thirty-Two

Each person in the room reacted separately to my announcement of my name. Molly frowned and glared, mixing anger and puzzlement at why I had chosen to answer their question in this way. Spud started opening and closing the loppers and moving towards Molly. Axel shifted his head back, with furrowed brows, and looked over to Craig.

And Craig had the look of someone whose rug had been ripped away from below his feet.

'Say that again,' Craig commanded.

'My name is Jake,' I said.

'Tell me more. Tell me everything,' said Craig.

Spud stopped moving towards Molly, and turned to face me.

'I think there's been a bit of a misunderstanding,' I said, trying to sound light and breezy. And failing.

'I'm Jake, not Pete. And I assume you're actually looking for him, only he's gone away. We're housemates.'

Craig paused, looked down, then let out a long sigh. He

stood up, walked to the end of the kitchen, and looked out of the window, before turning back to his men.

'Did no-one, and by no-one I specifically mean either of you, ever consider that it might be the teensiest bit helpful to actually get hold of the right person?'

Axel shrugged his shoulders. Spud lowered the loppers to his side, and said, 'We never met Pete. We only had this address. And this is the only person we've seen living here over the last couple of days.'

Craig cursed under his breath for a few seconds, and then more loudly for another few seconds.

'So where is Pete?' he asked.

'He went off to Wales. He said he was visiting his parents. Though he did leave without much warning. I was surprised.'

Craig cursed again.

'By the way,' I said to Axel, 'it's his rabbit, not mine.' Apparently, I was more worried by what a thug thought about my pet-keeping care than the fact I was still tied up with a friend with both of us facing violence.

Axel grunted, in a way in which I hoped indicated that his condemnation had somewhat lessened.

Craig stared for a second, decided to leave to one side whether now was the best time to bring up rabbits, and resumed his questioning.

'So Pete's cleared off and you've got no idea where it is?'

'I don't know... but I could have a guess.'

Craig looked a little more interested. 'Go on.'

'I assume your property is a type of...' I paused, trying to think of a suitable euphemism, 'grass?'

It wasn't much of a euphemism.

'Perhaps it is,' said Craig.

'Well, it might appeal to Pete's sense of humour to store grass in grass.'

Puzzlement shot across Craig's face, but Axel's lit up. He strode over to the big bag of hay next to the hutch, thrust his arm inside, and began to rummage. Little strands of hay began to float around the kitchen. One or two ended up on top of Mr B's cage, encouraging him to sit up and nibble bits through the ceiling of the hutch. Another few strands settled on Craig's trousers, to his irritation. He brushed them off with quick strokes of his hand. A second later, Axel withdrew his arm from the bag of hay, triumphantly clutching a package about the size of a brick wrapped in black plastic. He then repeated the process a couple of times, ending up with three black packages.

'All present and correct, boss.' Axel grinned. It was a shock seeing him with a happy face. Like seeing Snowdon without the summit in clouds but bathed in sunshine. You might know it was theoretically possible, but the reality was still a surprise.

Axel picked the black rucksack off the floor, and started putting the packages inside. Spud took a sip of tea, and then asked, 'so what do we do with these two?'

Craig smiled benevolently. 'As they've been so cooperative, and we've got what we've come for, I think we can let them go.'

'So no loppers? I've been dying to try them out.'

Craig paused, but then said, 'Not this time. Doesn't seem fair. Don't worry, you'll get a chance.'

Spud sighed, put the loppers in the black rucksack with the packages, and took another sip of his mug. I coughed, in what I hoped was a discreet but still enough to draw attention to our current predicament manner.

Spud sighed again, got up and went over to Molly.

'Now,' he said to her, 'I'm going to take the tape off your mouth. Don't do anything stupid like shouting, or I'll get me loppers again. Understood?'

Molly nodded.

He took one corner of the tape, and ripped it away from her face.

Although Molly didn't shout, to be fair there was quite a lot of loud 'Ow, ow, ow,' interspersed with some inventive cursing.

'Sorry about that,' said Spud, oozing a complete lack of sympathy.

'Now start cutting them free,' said Craig.

'Hang on, I'll see if there're any scissors.' Spud started rummaging through the kitchen drawers.

'How do you know we won't go to the police?' asked Molly. I wasn't sure it was the best question to ask, bringing up all sorts of reasons for them to hurt us again. But Craig seemed unput-out.

'Why would you? No harm, no foul.'

I decided not to point out GBH, breaking and entering, kidnapping and threatened violence. Molly took a different path.

'What about the breaking and entering, kidnapping us and threatening us with violence?' she said.

'Oh,' said Craig. 'We've never been asked before. It's not something we usually worry about. For a start, most of our interactions are with people who are criminally compromised. Also, we find that people value their health more than going to the police.'

Axel said, 'Also, most people value the health of their friends and family. Be a shame, for example, if anything should happen to your cousin.' This last comment was directed at Molly.

Molly blanched and fell back silent.

Craig frowned. 'You are in a different category from most people, though. You've made a very good point, Molly.'

He went behind me, reached into my left trouser pocket, and took out my iPhone. He held it in front of my face and swiped up. It unlocked, and he began to press and swipe on the screen.

'Here we go, under contacts. Mum and Dad. Only a mobile. Let's give them a ring.'

Molly and I looked at each other. Craig pressed on the screen, and we could hear the faint sound of the iPhone trying to ring, then connecting.

'Hello? Is that Jake's mum? Sorry to call like this, but he wants to send a parcel to you, and he's forgotten the post-code. I'm David, one of his friends.'

A pause.

'No, he's on the loo. I think he's got the runs. Doesn't look after himself properly, does he?'

Another pause.

'Yes, it is just like him to forget, isn't it.' Craig chuckled. 'Hold on, just writing it down. Could you give me the full address? Just to make sure?'

A further pause.

'No, I don't know. Hope it's something nice for you. Anyway, got to go. Lovely talking with you, Jake's mum.'

Craig turned off the phone and put it down on the table.

'Be a shame if anything happened to them, wouldn't it Jake? Your mum sounds lovely. And you need to post her a present.'

The point had been made, loud and clear. Tell the police, and say goodbye to friends and family.

Meanwhile, Spud uttered a small cheer of triumph, and waved around a pair of scissors he had found. He first cut through the cable ties holding Molly, and then mine. We remained seated, rubbing our wrists where the ties had cut in.

'I should have known you weren't Pete. You don't look like someone who goes clubbing,' said Craig.

I decided not to take offence. 'You're right. I rarely go.'

'So what do you do?' he asked.

'I work with ancient papyri at the John Rylands Library in the centre of town. Stuff dug up from Egypt from two thousand years ago.'

'I made papyri in school,' said Spud. 'We were doing the ancient Egyptians. You got strips of brown paper, a bowl of glue, and made a lattice. Then we wrote our names in hiero-glyphics.'

I was about to explain that my papyri didn't use hiero-glyphs, when Axel said, 'His papyri will be ancient Greek. The hieroglyphic period was much earlier.'

We all turned round to stare at him.

He shrugged his shoulders. 'I like to read. And I some-times spend time off in places like John Rylands and the Manchester Museum.'

'My daughter's into all that stuff,' said Craig. 'Her school are planning an exhibition later in the year.'

Spud said, 'There was a story in the papers about a papyri. Some nerd stole it from a museum.'

'That nerd would be me,' I said.

Craig, Axel and Spud all looked at me. I couldn't be sure,

but it appeared that alongside the surprise was also an element of me climbing in their estimation.

'Not that I did steal it,' I added, 'I just got accused of it. That's why I thought at first you were looking for the papyrus, and why I thought you turned over the place on Monday.'

My admission that I hadn't actually stolen the papyrus lowered their estimation of me back down.

'Are they worth lots, then, these papyri?' asked Craig.

Axel intervened. 'A fragment of Romans sold for half a million dollars a year or two back. Mind you, technically that wasn't papyrus, it was vellum.'

'Vellum?' asked Spud.

'High quality paper,' said Axel. 'It's a type of carefully prepared animal skin. Like a thin leather.'

'Romans?' asked Craig.

'Bit of the Bible. Saint Paul's letter to the Romans.'

'We're in the wrong business, lads,' said Craig.

'So what exactly do you do?' asked Axel.

I explained that I was working my way through a box of unsorted and uncatalogued papyri.

'Tell you what you want to be doing. Using AI to do all that. If they can use it to read that stuff in Pompeii, why can't you use it on your stuff?'

He had a point. Researchers had recently managed to use AI to decipher a scroll that had been carbonised in volcanic ash at Herculaneum, in the same disaster that destroyed Pompeii. Any attempts to unroll it would have resulted in it falling apart, but a mixture of CT scanning and AI had managed to reveal its secrets.

'Not quite there yet, maybe in a few years.'

'So you work with all this type of stuff all day long,' asked Craig.

I nodded.

'You could help with my daughter's exhibition. They could do with a proper nerd helping them. If you don't get done for nicking the missing one.'

'My work may have something to say about my commitments,' I said, hoping to avoid further involvement with Craig and his two henchmen.

'No problem. Right, we'd best be off, then,' said Craig. 'Tell your friend Pete not to come back to Manchester if he values his limbs. We're not pleased with him.'

Axel turned to face me square on. 'That means the rabbit is yours now. Start taking proper care of him. I might be minded to check on him, make sure you're treating him right.'

I gulped, and agreed to take care of Mr B.

'Thanks for the tea. You alright if we leave you to do the washing up?' asked Spud.

'You're fine,' I reassured him. The three moved out of the kitchen, into the hall, pausing by the open doors off the hall to Pete's room and mine.

'Good book collection,' said Axel, looking into my room. I thanked him.

'Good posters. I like Tarantino,' said Craig, looking into Pete's room. I didn't tell him they were Pete's.

As they reached the door, Spud and Axel left the house first. Craig paused on the doorstep, and turned around. He reached into his jacket, and for an awful second I thought he was going to pull out a gun.

Instead, he drew out a fifty-pound note. As he held it in his fingertips in front of him, he said, 'I feel a bit bad. It's obvious you and the girl have nothing to do with this. Here, have a meal on me.'

And he took my right hand, and thrust the note into it.

'Be seeing ya,' he said, and walked off into the street.

I closed the door behind them, leant back against it, and let out a sigh of relief before walking back to the kitchen. Molly was standing up, stretching her arms, with a scowl on her face.

She glowered at me, and said, 'this is the worst date I've ever been on.'

Chapter Thirty-Three

'Sorry,' I said. It seemed necessary, under the circumstances. The date could hardly be said to have gone well. I wasn't surprised it was her worst. It was at least in the top three of the worst dates I had been on.

'They threatened to cut off my fingers. With a lopper. If I ever meet Pete, he'll be lucky if it's just his fingers I cut off.'

I noticed the focus of her anger was more aimed at Pete rather than me, and decided it might be wise to go with her flow.

'Yeah, what's that about, leaving us to deal with his mess. Typical.'

'And why on earth do you live with a drug dealer? That makes your house a drug den.'

The focus was shifting dangerously back to me.

'I didn't have a clue he was dealing. I knew he smoked weed – his room always stinks of it.'

'Now I don't know what to think. You're messing around with drug gangs, and a valuable papyrus goes missing. Maybe you do have a motive for nicking it.' Molly turned away from me, and glanced around the kitchen. She bent down and picked up a couple of stray bits of hay that had fallen to the floor near her chair, then moved over to the kitchen units, opening them until she found a bin.

'Come on,' I said, trying to sound convincing, 'they thought I was Pete. They'd never even heard of me, they didn't know who I was. They didn't even know I'd been in the papers.'

'Hmm.'

She still wasn't looking at me.

I drove home my point. 'And why would I bother trekking all around Manchester if I had the papyrus in the first place?'

This turned out to be a tactical error. Another frown flitted across her face, and she said, 'Oh, I don't know, I suppose I was under the illusion that you might like my company. But no, it's all about the papyrus. Silly me.'

'But that was the point of investigating...' I said.

'Don't worry, you've made it clear what was important today and what wasn't. Papyrus, important. Molly, not so much. You couldn't wait to tell them I wasn't your girlfriend.'

'But you're not my girlfriend,' I said, ensuring that, like buses, saying exactly the wrong thing comes in threes.

'Thanks for making that clear as crystal. There are countless bells less clear than that. It is so clear, it's visible from outer space. Maybe you'd like to shove it further down my throat? As far as my stomach, will that do?'

The situation needed rescuing quickly.

'I didn't like to presume. And I thought the less they thought we were linked, the less obvious it was how much I like you, the less likely they were to hurt you.'

'Oh,' Molly said, and fell silent for a few seconds. Then

she looked back at me as she continued, 'So you were trying to be indifferent?'

'I couldn't let them know how much I like you–' I stopped, realising what I was saying. I could feel my cheeks and ears burning, and hoped they weren't also turning red.

'You're blushing,' Molly said, beginning to smile. My cheeks turned up the temperature another notch. There's nothing like being told you're blushing to keep you blushing.

'No I'm not,' I lied.

'So you did enjoy going around Manchester today?'

'I did. If this was a date, then until we got tied up and threatened with extreme violence, it was going really well from my point of view. Badly, from the papyrus point of view. But good, from the date point of view.'

'You weren't sure if this was a date? But I said it was a date.'

'You said, "it's a date," but sometimes people say that just to confirm a meeting or time. I didn't want to misread signals.'

I picked up the mugs, and took them to the sink, and turned on the hot tap.

'Hold on,' Molly said, 'shouldn't we keep those as evidence for the police? DNA from their mouths?'

'You think we should go to the police over this?'

'They threatened us. Isn't that what the police is for?'

I paused, wondering myself what the best plan would be.

'They didn't actually hurt us, but they could still hurt either of us or Maisy. And my parents. They know where you work, and they know where I work – or at least used to work. We'd probably have to go into witness protection for a while, so you couldn't take up your job.'

'Witness protection? I thought that was an American thing.'

'No, Britain has it too. I knew someone who spent a couple of years in witness protection. He said it was boring. He got moved to a small, terraced house in another city, and couldn't contact friends or family. He gave up in the end and just moved back home and took the risks there.'

'How do you know people in witness protection?'

'I volunteered at a youth club near Moss Side for a couple of years. It was one of the other volunteers.'

'Another city and no contact with family...' Molly's voice trailed off, and she looked down at the floor.

'And if we go to the police, Pete is going to be arrested too.'

'I'm not sure I care about Pete. I know he's your friend, but look what a mess he left us in.'

'And Craig was almost nice at the end,' I added.

'At the end, after nearly cutting off various body parts. How was he nice?'

I held up the fifty pound note still in my hand. 'He gave us this to have a meal out for our troubles.'

Molly pouted. 'I feel contaminated by this. Okay, we don't go to the police. But I think I've had enough for the day. I want to go home now.'

My heart sank. This wasn't how I had envisaged the date (now I was sure it had been a date) ending.

'I'll get you an Uber,' I said, getting out my phone. 'Also, I think I know what happened with the papyrus.'

Chapter Thirty-Four

Molly said, 'what?' and furrowed her eyebrows.

'I think I know what happened. I just need to work out what to do about it,' I said. 'What's your address for the Uber?'

'Never mind the Uber, you can't just tell me you've sorted everything out and then pack me off in a taxi.'

I paused, and glanced at the fifty-pound note in my hand. My head still had a dull throbbing sensation. 'Are you sure you'd feel contaminated if we spent this on food? Also, do you mind holding on while I find some paracetamol? My head's aching.'

'Why?' asked Molly.

'Because I'm getting a bit hungry, and I think better if I have some food every now and then.'

'No, why have you got a headache?'

I realised that Molly had been at the shops when I had been jumped by Axel and Spud, and had only seen me once I was already tied to the chair and awake.

'They knocked me out, just outside my front door. Hit me on the back of the head. I woke up trussed on the chair.'

I went over to one of the kitchen cupboards where Pete sometimes kept medicines, and started to poke around. I could only see some Strepsils and a bottle of Gaviscon. Both looked as if they had been there a while.

I turned round to find Molly with eyes and mouth both wide open.

'You've had a concussion?' she said. 'How long were you out for?'

'I don't know, only a few minutes. I was awake by the time you got back from the shop.'

'Yes, but even a short concussion can be dangerous.' She appraised me, looking me up and down, as though expecting me to fall down any second.

'I'm half expecting you to fall down any second,' she said. 'This is serious. Where's my phone?'

'It's over by the chair you were in. Axel had it. Or was it Spud? Anyway, I feel fine apart from the headache. It doesn't feel serious.'

'It could lead to a brain thingy. You know.' Molly leapt to her phone.

'Well, that sounds worrying. A thingy.'

Molly didn't answer; she was tapping rapidly on her mobile, before pausing and reading the screen.

'I'm just going to find the paracetamol,' I said, turning towards the hallway and the stairs. 'I think it's in the bathroom.'

'A and E. Straight away. Where's the nearest hospital?'

'Seems a bit much. And I'll be there ages. Down in a sec,' I said, continuing up the stairs.

I found a pack of paracetamol capsules in the bathroom

cabinet. There were still six left, so I popped two out, and started back downstairs.

'No, we're going to hospital. It says to on the NHS page.'

I sighed, and carried on into the kitchen, and turned on the tap. I found a glass, and swallowed both the tablets.

'The MRI is the closest. The one we passed on the bus. But you wait forever in those places unless you're bleeding to death. Can't we go and get some food? There's a really nice Greek takeaway just a couple of hundred yards away, before Sainsbury's, and they've got a couple of tables inside you can eat at.'

'Nope. Not on my watch. I'm calling an Uber. And you need something cold to put on the swelling.'

I sighed, and opened up the freezer. In one drawer was a pack of frozen sweetcorn. I took it out and placed it on the back of my neck.

'That's good,' Molly said encouragingly. 'It says to do that on the NHS page.'

'Put sweetcorn on your neck?'

'Frozen peas. But it's the same thing, isn't it? Three minutes for the Uber.'

I sighed again.

'Stop sighing. It's happening.' Molly didn't have the softest bedside manner.

'Okay, but let me get a couple of things first.'

'The Uber's almost here. What do you need?'

'A power bank for the phone. A really long novel.'

Molly laughed. 'Stop sounding miserable. You need checking, and that's it. Grab the power bank. But I'm coming along too.'

I prepared to sigh again, and then stopped. At least if Molly was alongside me, the hospital wait wouldn't be quite so dull. I went into my study, and picked up a power bank and charging cable.

Molly called from the front door, 'It's here. Time to go.'

'I need to sort Mr B. Hold on.'

I went back into the kitchen and checked that Mr B had plenty of hay and water. I didn't want to feel the wrath of Axel again. Then I went out, locked up, and prepared for a fun evening in waiting rooms.

Chapter Thirty-Five

'Okay, I think you've been lucky. I can't see any obvious danger signs, and you're responding fine to my questions,' said the doctor.

His name was Doctor Linden. He looked about the same age as me. Around his neck he wore the obligatory stethoscope. He had been blessed with classic good looks: high cheekbones; rugged chin; short, neatly cut blond hair and eyes so blue you could swim in them. He was finishing his examination of me, having checked both physical symptoms (nausea, vomiting?) and mental acuity (who is the prime minister, any memory lapses?), along with my condition since the concussion.

'That's great, isn't it, Doctor Linden?' said Molly. I was sitting on a hospital bed, near the pillows, and Molly was perched at the other end, legs crossed. We were in a bay in the accident and emergency unit at the Royal Infirmary, with a blue curtain pulled around to give us a degree of privacy while being seen to. The privacy only extended to sight; snatched conversations from the other bays echoed around if patients spoke loudly. Some did, of prolapsed bowels, of chest pains, and in one case of an earring that was stuck. The background stories, along with the temperature bring slightly too warm and a smell of disinfectant covering up fainter odours of blood and vomit, made sure you knew you were in hospital.

'It's certainly seems like good news. I don't think we need a scan unless you develop any further symptoms, Jake,' said Doctor Linden.

Molly ran her hand through her hair. 'What do we need to look out for?'

Doctor Linden turned towards her, and she smiled. Almost as if she was flirting with him. Which she couldn't be, I told myself.

'You might get some nausea or headaches. If they don't go away within two weeks, contact your GP. No drugs or alcohol. Try to get plenty of rest, and avoid stressful situations. If you start vomiting, or a headache that paracetamol doesn't work for, or memory problems, come straight back here.'

I wondered how I was meant to avoid stress.

Molly said, 'And that's everything?'

'One more thing,' said the doctor, and turned to Molly. 'Jake will need someone around him for the next twenty-four hours. Particularly tonight. Will that be a problem?'

Molly came in straight away. 'Oh, I'm not his girlfriend.' She said it firmly, and with a hint of smugness. 'I'm single.'

Doctor Linden seemed a little taken aback. 'Sorry, I shouldn't have presumed.'

Molly reached out, touched his hand, and said, 'No need to apologise.'

Definitely flirting.

'I'm sure I'll be fine,' I said. 'The headache is going now, mostly, anyway.'

The doctor looked uncertain. 'I'd be much happier if you could find someone to stay with you overnight. Is there anyone you could phone?'

'Is that really necessary?' I said.

'Yes, it's necessary. Could you stay with a friend?'

Molly sighed. 'I can stay overnight.'

'You don't have to do that,' I said.

'I know. But I'd feel bad if something happened to you. I'll stay.'

The doctor smiled. 'That's great, then. I'll get the discharge paperwork sorted. You get a copy, and a copy goes to your GP. Good to meet you, Jake and Molly.' He drew back the blue curtain, disappeared through the gap, and then from the other side drew the curtain closed again.

'You seemed to like the doctor,' I said.

'I don't know how he's allowed in hospital. His cheek-bones are so sharp they're practically lethal weapons. And those big, big blue eyes... people could drown in them.'

'Just as well you're not my girlfriend, then,' I said, a shade grumpily.

'You've been telling people all day I'm not your girl-friend. I thought I'd have a turn.'

I sniffed in protest, and fell quiet, leaving a clamour of conversations and the discordant bleeping of medical machinery to fill the silence. Then I added, 'But thanks for agreeing to stay the night.'

'Never mind tonight, maybe you need to rethink your plans for tomorrow,' said Molly, 'as luscious Doctor Linden said to avoid stress.'

During our time in the waiting room, I had filled Molly

in with what I thought had happened, and everything that I was hoping to do on the Thursday. It couldn't be described as calm or stress-free.

'I don't think I've got a choice,' I said, ignoring the comment about Doctor Linden. The board are meeting on Friday, and the handover is tomorrow evening. This isn't something I can postpone.'

Doctor Linden came back into the bay, holding a couple of sheets of paper in his right hand, which he offered to me. 'You're free to go. Remember to rest and contact us if you get those symptoms we discussed. Here's your discharge letter, and here's a leaflet on head injuries.'

I thanked him, and took the leaflets. Molly smiled at him, and also thanked him. Once he had left the bay again, she jumped off the end of the bed, turned to me, and said, 'I'll call an Uber. It's time you were in bed.'

Chapter Thirty-Six

The Uber deposited us outside my house. I looked carefully around the street. Just the usual cars, litter, the smell of takeaways and a cat delicately making its way along the pavement. There was nothing ominous at all. I opened the door, and we entered the house again, me making sure I locked the door behind us, and we went through to the kitchen. It was bizarre that just hours ago we had been tied up and threatened. It felt like a dream I had had, except a bump on the back of my head and cut cable ties on the floor showed it had been very real.

'Do you have any food in the house?' asked Molly. 'I'm starving.'

The vending machine in the waiting room at the MRI had been broken.

'We could still walk to the Greek takeaway down the road,' I said.

'Nah. I can't be bothered, and you should be resting,' said Molly. She wandered over to the fridge, and opened it up.

'You've got some eggs in here. And spinach. And four cans of Stella. Classy.'

'The Stella is Pete's. Or was, if he's not coming back. And the spinach is for the rabbit.'

'Neither of them is in a position to say no to us, so poached eggs on toast with some spinach it is.'

I moved towards the cupboards, and suddenly felt my balance slipping away. I stopped, and grabbed hold of the back of a chair. Molly frowned, and gestured for me to sit down. I did. The events of the day were beginning to catch up with me. I pulled the chair over to the table, and sat there with my head supported by my hands, elbows on the table. I closed my eyes for a second.

'Here you go. Eggs are ready,' said Molly. I opened my eyes with a start.

'You've had a mini nap. Eat up, then it's bed time.' She put a plate and cutlery in front of me, fetched hers, and sat down at the table. Then she got up, closed the kitchen door, and opened up Mr B's cage before sitting down again. He sniffed suspiciously, then hopped out, and began exploring the kitchen.

'Don't want Axel to get angry again, do we,' said Molly, and smiled. She threw a small handful of uncooked spinach onto the kitchen floor, and Mr B started chomping on it.

I looked down at my plate, felt a wave of nausea coming on, and pushed it away. 'Sorry, just don't fancy anything at the moment.'

Molly was making rapid inroads into her plate. She nodded to acknowledge she had heard, and carried on eating. Meanwhile, Mr B had come over to me, and was rubbing his chin on my shoe. I bent down to stroke him. For a couple of seconds he stayed still, letting me stroke him, then he stretched, and hopped off back into his cage.

'Do you think Pete will come back?' asked Molly.

'I don't know,' I replied. 'I think he left in a hurry because he knew he'd got in over his head. He might come to collect his things, but beyond that I haven't a clue. I'll text him tomorrow and find out more.'

'Will he take the rabbit?'

'Dunno,' I said, 'I think he got Mr B on a whim. I came home one day, and Pete had just bought him off some bloke he'd met. Actually, looking back, he may have been high when he got him.'

Mr B ignored the talk about him, and stretched out, half-closing his eyes, ears flopped either side of his head. I wondered whether I would end up owning a rabbit. And how long they lived. And whether you needed insurance. And Axel had suggested another rabbit, and letting them have more space. I frowned again.

'I think you ought to cancel everything tomorrow. You look rubbish. I've seen goths with more colour than you.'

I shook my head. 'I need to do stuff. It won't wait.'

Molly stood up and cleared our plates.

'It's getting late,' she said, emptying my plate into the bin before depositing both of them into the sink.

I stood up, checked that Mr B still had enough water and hay, and closed the lid on his hutch.

Molly turned around, and moved closer to me, facing me. She reached around the back of her head, and removed a hair band, shaking her hair loose. A stray strand fell across her right eye. In a soft, breathy voice, she said, 'I don't normally stay the night on a first date. But you've got me into your bed, Doctor Andrews.'

Then she grinned, and in a normal voice added, 'I don't know where you're going to sleep, mind. Are you taking your chances on Pete's bedding, or the sofa?'

Chapter Thirty-Seven

I looked up and down Deansgate again, trying to spot Professor Chelworth amongst the throng of passers-by. I had arrived early, and I was now nervously waiting outside Caffè Nero.

I had chosen to kip on the sofa last night (the thought of what Pete's bed might harbour was grim), and had slept fitfully, until woken by Molly presenting me with a mug of tea. She was already dressed, and her hair was pulled back into a rough ponytail.

'How are you feeling? Any nausea?'

I shook my head. I felt a little queasy, but better than the previous night. My head still ached, but it had descended to a duller, background pain.

'Okay, I have to get home, and shower and change into fresh clothes. The Uber's almost here. Maybe see you later.'

I sat up, grabbed the mug, and I smiled at her, and she smiled at me, then she patted my hand, and left. I could hear the front door open and close through the hallway.

I tried to decipher what the pat on the hand had meant.

Was it like a nurse, or a friend, or something more? Then I decided I was overthinking it, and forced myself off the sofa. Half an hour, a shower, a shave, two paracetamol, one fed rabbit and a slice of toast later, I was out of the house, and heading for the bus stop.

And now I was waiting to have a meeting to decide my future.

A steady stream of pedestrians flowed around me. Young men and women in sharp suits, talking loudly as they headed into city centre offices. A couple of mothers or childminders pushing buggies. A mix of people in casual attire. A couple of teenage girls in black hijabs, Adidas sportswear and New Balance trainers giggling together. A Big Issue seller walking to their spot. The usual eclectic mix of a Manchester midweek morning.

Occasionally I would fix on a person, and wonder what was going on in their lives. All of their hopes, dreams, and fears, so central to them, and yet invisible to me.

'Mate, can you move a bit? You're blocking half the pavement.' A thin man with lanky hair, torn jeans and holding a reefer took me out of my philosophical musings. I apologised and moved closer to the wall. I checked the time on my phone. Still five minutes to go before 10am.

And then I finally spotted him, navigating his way along the street. Professor Chelworth was dressed in his usual array of browns: tweed jacket, shiny brown brogues and dark brown trousers. Even his tie was brown, made from wool with diagonal checks. He looked like a fanboy for an Edwardian comeback movement. Rather an unhappy fanboy: his face was scowling.

'Professor, over here,' I said, waving an arm.

He looked up at me, and continued scowling. 'I know

where you are, you're quite visible. And I know where the café is. I'm not an idiot.'

'Sorry, just wanted to make sure you'd seen me. Thanks for making the time today, can we go in and talk over a coffee? I'll buy.'

He grunted in response. Then he walked ahead of me into the café, saying, 'Let's get this over with. I'll buy. You need all the help you can get.'

'Thanks,' I said, following him in.

It took a couple of seconds for my eyes to adjust to the darker interior of Caffè Nero. The professor was almost camouflaged against the dark brown walls. The comforting sound of grinding beans and the splutter of steam provided a backdrop of coffee-related sounds, above which bubbled the occasional murmurs of quiet conversation.

The tables inside were already mostly taken. One near the back had been commandeered by a harassed looking man with sleeves rolled up and tie hanging loose who had settled in for the day, with laptops, piles of paper, caffeine and stress lines as his surroundings of choice. Near the door, a woman dressed in smart white shirt, a short, patterned skirt and knee-high leather boots was browsing through the Metro, her coat slung casually across the back of the other chair. The next table along featured a tall black man in casual clothes, with white AirPods, sipping an espresso from a takeaway cup and scrolling through his phone. The next two tables also featured people filtering the world through AirPods: a woman in her thirties or forties facing away and hunched over, as though trying to shut the universe out whilst scribbling furiously in a note-book, and a younger woman with brown hair with a tall flat white.

Professor Chelworth gave his order at the counter. 'Espresso. And what do you want, Jake?'

'Americano, cold skimmed milk on the side.'

The professor got out his phone to register reward points, and to pay, and looked around the room.

'It's busy. Don't know if we'll get a seat.'

But as he said this, the tall black man yawned, stretched, and unfolded himself from his chair. He gave us a smile, and walked out, taking his cup and depositing it in the bin. I gratefully sat down at one of the two chairs. The professor remained near the counter, waiting for our drinks. He glanced over as I checked my phone, before putting it back down on the table.

'Do you need sugar?' he asked.

I shook my head. 'I'm good.'

The drinks appeared, and the professor took them on a tray, before placing each cup separately on our round table, then the milk for my Americano, before dropping the tray to the side of his chair. He sat down, with his mouth down-turned and gazing at me with sad eyes.

'Well, this is most regrettable. I don't really know how you think I can help you. It's all down to the trustees, and until this nastiness is resolved...' He grimaced, and then took a sip of espresso.

I added some milk to my drink and took a gulp. The bitter-sweet acidity started its journey through my body. Then I placed the large white cup back down carefully next to my phone. I straightened up, held eye contact, and asked my question in a quiet, yet clear voice.

'Why did you steal the papyrus, Professor Chelworth?'

Chapter Thirty-Eight

Professor Chelworth had started picking up his espresso, but he stopped, holding it in mid-air. His eyebrows shot up, and he started back slightly. He said nothing.

Then his eyes narrowed, he looked around the café, and placed his cup back on the table. He tilted his head to one side, a bird of prey considering a threat. Then he leant forward, and turned over my phone.

We both looked at it. The voice memo app showed a red button in a grey circle, with a timer running above it. A spectrum displayed a visual representation of the sound of the café. The professor stretched out his right index finger, touched the red button, and the phone bleeped, showing a new recording had been stored. Then he raised his index finger, wagging it side to side.

'I don't think we need to record anything,' he said. He glanced again around the café, and then settled back into his chair, confidence returning.

I slumped in mine. The plan to record a confession on my iPhone had already failed.

'But why did you do it?' I asked.

'What makes you think I did?' he said. Both of us were aware that he hadn't denied it.

'I put it all together. I was confused at first, because I thought stuff happening at home had to do with the papyrus. But when I realised it didn't, then it had to be you. It wasn't the American Brad Ryan. He wants to buy the fragment, so he didn't take it. The three Manchester clergy are unlikely. Two of them got dragged into it. And what would they do with it? The Italian priest was one of the first to leave my room. That leaves me, Maisy and you. I know I didn't take it, and I know Maisy wouldn't take it.'

'How clever. I'm surprised,' he said. I ignored the insult.

'Again, why did you do it?'

Professor Chelworth looked incredulous, as though a small child had asked what two plus two made.

'For the money, of course. Why else would anyone do it?'

'But you're a professor. Surely you don't need money enough to do... ...this?'

His mouth settled into a hard line, and he furrowed his eyebrows.

'I get paid a pittance.' He practically spat the words out. 'A pittance. My friends at university, who went into banking, do you know what they're on?'

I shook my head. I had no idea how much bankers earned, except it was a lot more than me.

'One of my friends has a holiday home in Bermuda. And he's thick – thick as custard. He's on a million quid a year, and I'm on one hundred and twenty. Where's the justice?'

Where was the justice was a fair question, I allowed,

considering that I, a world expert in my field with a PhD, was on a temporary contract paid about a quarter of the professor's salary.

'But why risk it all for an extra hundred thousand pounds?'

'A hundred thousand?' The professor looked puzzled.

'The American came to me. That's the number he was talking about.'

The professor laughed.

'He saw you coming. A hundred thousand is chump change. I'm getting two million.'

'Two million pounds?' The amount shocked me.

'For a unique papyrus, with secure provenance and date. The earliest Christian fragment we have. And a fragment that could change our understanding of the gospels and the early church. For a museum desperate to have some prestige. They snapped at the offer.'

I sat back, taking in the information for a second. The professor took another sip of his espresso.

'How did you do it?' I asked.

'You weren't meant to transcribe and read it. I needed it authenticated as part of the Grove collection so that its provenance and date were secure. Once it was catalogued, it would go missing, and no-one would notice. Not for years, maybe even decades.'

I nodded. This was what I had thought. His scheme had simplicity on its side. Each museum hosting papyri collections often has hundreds or thousands of fragments which no-one has got around to examining closely. And if someone had stumbled upon the photograph or catalogue entry, the trail of the missing papyrus would be colder than Antarctica. The American museum would get an authenticated

187

papyrus; the John Rylands wouldn't even notice what had gone.

'And then you came along and spoiled everything. Why couldn't you just do your job?'

'How did you take it?'

'I palmed it as we left your office,' he said. 'It's easy with a small fragment.'

'And the papyrus fragment in my bag?' I asked.

'I slipped it in once I knew you had called the police. I thought it might draw more attention to you and create a bit of confusion. If I'm honest, I almost panicked a bit when you told us you had read it, and this seemed like a good idea at the time,' he said, and he shrugged his shoulders.

I looked away from him in disgust and anger. Around us, the café continued its hubbub, and outside the window pedestrians continued to wander past, a world oblivious to this confession.

'How could you do it?' I asked. 'How could you ruin my life?'

He shrugged again. 'Collateral damage. Someone had to take the blame, once you called in the police. In a way it's your fault for not just doing what you were asked. After tomorrow you won't be in academia anymore in any case. It might even do you good. You could try for a banking job yourself.' Any trace of concern for me had disappeared from his face some time ago.

'So the decision by the trustees has already been made?'

'It's a formality. I'm about to send them my recommendation. Bye bye to Jake Andrews. Hello to some new post-doc who will snap my hand off at the chance to work on this project.'

'But what if I tell them the truth?'

'The truth? They can't handle the truth,' he said, and then laughed.

'You're hardly one of a few good men,' I said, not joining in with his hilarity.

'More to the point,' he replied, 'no-one is going to believe you. You're the prime suspect, trying to pass the blame. You have no evidence, I will deny everything, and everyone will assume you're trying to wriggle your way out of your own crimes. Still, with the papyrus missing and with no photograph, it looks like you won't necessarily go to prison. Not enough evidence. Silver lining and all that.'

'I still don't know how you could do it. You've devoted your entire life to studying papyrology, and here is a once in a generation find, unique, important, and you want to flog it to an American nutter with a dodgy library.'

The professor moved back in his chair again. Then he began to chuckle. It was a sound that started low and rumbled, and gradually built into a crescendo of laughter. It was loud enough that the harassed man at the last table looked up briefly from his laptop, before returning to spreadsheets.

'My dear boy,' he said, speaking quietly while wiping tears of laughter from his eyes, 'you didn't think the papyrus was genuine, did you?'

Chapter Thirty-Nine

I took a few seconds to digest what the professor had said. Meanwhile, he resumed sipping his espresso.

'The coffee's not bad here,' he said, 'I should come here more often.'

While my mind was whirling, the rest of world carried on as usual. The woman by the door flicked over another page of her newspaper. The harassed man started typing furiously on his laptop. A loud grinding noise promised more fresh coffee.

'Fake? It's a fake papyrus?'

'But now, if you'll excuse me, I have a recommendation for the trustees to write up. Got to think of the reputation of the institution. I can't stay long.'

'How do you know it's a fake?' I asked.

He smiled, looking smug. In his face you could see the battle between ducking out of the conversation, and proving how much cleverer he was than me. Pride won.

'Because I made it. I was worried it was a bit too obvious.

But you've just proved you can't go wrong underestimating your colleagues.'

'But how? How did you forge it?'

'Easy enough. When the collection first came in, I skimmed through it in case anything interesting stood out straight away. And a couple of small fragments were bare. Nothing on them at all. At first, I thought I could use them in a workshop with students. But then, I had a better idea. I just wrote something enticing on one of them and told the yanks I had something desirable. Easy.'

He put down his cup, and sat back in his chair, legs crossed. I began to work out how Professor Chelworth thought he would get away with the deceit.

'So the actual papyrus does date from the first century,' I said, thinking aloud, 'and that early date makes it easier, because you were trying to replicate carbon black ink rather than iron gall.'

Professor Chelworth tilted his head, looked at me and smiled.

'Because carbon black ink doesn't eat into the papyrus,' I said, continuing to air my thoughts. 'If you'd tried to imitate iron gall ink, it would be easier to see that it had been applied recently. You'd expect the acid to have affected the papyrus. And with carbon black ink, you didn't have to worry about it not looking faded.'

Continuing to smile, the professor took off his tortoise-shell glasses, and began to wipe them clean on his tie.

'And then, if anyone did try and date the papyrus,' I continued, 'carbon-14 dating would give the right century. The result would say, yes, these fibres come from the middle of the first century, plus or minus fifty years. And no-one carbon dates the ink, because it destroys the sample. And the ink, if you've followed a simple recipe, would also pass Raman spectroscopy.'

Raman spectroscopy was a relatively new technology for papyrology. Without destroying any of the sample, it could tell you the chemical components of a material. It had been used to work out the ingredients in ancient inks, and to authenticate a range of artworks and ancient artefacts.

'And if it's going to a private museum who shouldn't have this fragment in the first place, they're not going to get a lot of experts to examine it closely to tell if it's forged or real.'

The professor gave me a slow, sarcastic hand clap.

'The hardest thing,' he said, 'was getting the script right. I didn't want some palaeographer saying this wasn't the style used in that period.'

'What did you use as an exemplar?' I asked.

'The wet nurse contract. P.rein 2.103. Lots of text and about the right date.'

He was referring to a papyrus that the Sorbonne had in their collection. It was a contract dated to AD 26 agreeing terms for a woman to wetnurse a baby for a couple of years before returning the child to be reared as a slave. You could access high resolution images of the papyrus freely online.

'Did you worry about ink flow on the papyrus?' I asked.

'I did, but the fragment is relatively flat, and I guessed that, since they weren't meant to have it in the first place, they wouldn't be in a position to get any other expert to check that level of detail.'

Over time, papyri can warp. The ink, if original, warps with the fibre. If applied centuries later, it flows to the wrong places, filling in and pooling in places where it shouldn't. It was a tell that had exposed some forgeries as fakes. It was one of the signs that had led to another recent sensational find, implying that Jesus was married, being exposed as a modern fake.

'Where did you get the reed pen from?' I asked.

'They sell bundles of them on Amazon. I got a packet when I was doing a workshop with some students last year.'

The professor leant forward, picked up his espresso cup, and drained it.

'This has been delightful,' he said. 'It's actually nice to be able to tell someone about it. And at least you can appreciate some of the finer points.'

'Yes, delightful.'

He placed his cup delicately back down on its saucer, picked up a paper napkin, and wiped either side of his mouth.

'Such a shame,' he said, napkin still in hand, 'that your little recording ploy didn't work.'

He went to stand up, but the woman closest to the door got up at the same time, and she bumped into him. He sat down again, apologising.

'Oh, don't apologise, I think it was my fault.' the woman said. And then, 'Professor Chelworth, Jemma Williamson here. You've just admitted to a massive fraud. Do you have any comment for readers of the Manchester Evening Standard?'

Chapter Forty

The professor's eyes widened, and his mouth fell open. Blood drained from his face.

'Wha– what?' he said, and nervously laughed.

'The Manchester Evening Standard. Would you like to comment further on your actions?'

'But... but... you can't have heard much.' His hands gripped the base of his chair, as he sought to regain control. 'It's a noisy café. I don't know what you think you've heard, but you're mistaken.'

'If only,' I said, 'we had some type of recording.'

'Yes, well, there is no recording.' But as he said it, doubt crept into his face. He glanced down at my iPhone, still on the table, looked up at me, and then grabbed it.

The iPhone had gone into sleep mode, and now it asked him for a passcode. He tossed it back onto the table, where it landed with a clatter. I winced, and hoped that the case I kept my phone in had protected it.

'No comment,' said the professor, more firmly now. 'You've got no evidence. I've nothing to say to the press, and if you try to print anything accusing me of fraud, I shall sue. And now, I think I had better be on my way.' He made to get up again.

At that moment, the younger woman two tables away got up. The harassed man stopped typing, and looked up, beginning to be intrigued by what was going on. The woman walked over to our table.

'Oh, sorry,' she said, 'I was here earlier, and I think I left something.'

She reached under the table, and pulled out a small black box with a black wire coming out leading to a miniature microphone. Still attached to the black box were a couple of long strips of masking tape. A small green LED light glowed on the end of the black box.

'Ah, here it is. One of my radio mikes. Oh, look, it was on all this time. How careless of me.'

The professor watched all this with amazement, mouth slack again.

'You need to be more careful of your stuff, Molly,' I said, 'next thing you'll be telling me is that you accidentally recorded everything.'

'You may be right, Jake. Do you know, I think I did.' Molly smiled at me.

The professor looked wildly back and forth between Molly, Jemma and me.

'You can't... who is this...?' he stammered.

'Molly is a friend of mine who works in audio,' I said. 'It looks like we do have a recording after all.'

The professor took a deep breath, and then another.

'You can't use it,' he said. 'It's illegal to record someone without their consent. GDPR and all that. You can't use it in a court of law.'

By this stage, the harassed man had stopped looking harassed, and had also stopped worrying about his work, at least for now. He was rapt with attention. Meanwhile, the older woman on the table between our table and Molly's stopped writing into her notebook and turned around.

'That's not quite accurate,' she said to the professor, 'I think you may be thinking of some US states. Here in England the courts can admit covert recordings if they believe them to be helpful and reliable.'

'I've met you,' said the professor, staring wide-eyed at the woman.

'Yes, earlier this week. I'm DS Penry. And alongside the recording that Molly took, I've been making contemporaneous notes of the conversation from what I could hear sitting next to you.'

The professor slumped back and his whole body sagged.

'To confirm, I am DS Penry, a sergeant with the Manchester Metropolitan Police force.'

Outside the window, I could see that a uniformed officer had arrived, with DC Rushton by his side. Both were now waiting by the door.

'Professor Richard Chelworth, I am arresting you because I have reasonable grounds to believe you have committed theft and fraud. You will now be detained and taken to a police station. You do not have to say anything. But, it may harm your defence if you do not mention when questioned something which you later rely on in court. Anything you do say may be given in evidence. Please stand up so my colleague DC Rushton can search you.'

The professor, looking bewildered, stood up, and DC Rushton came into the café. Wearing a pair of latex gloves, he searched through the professor's jacket, while the professor remained standing, arms outstretched. Jemma used her phone to get some pictures. The formerly harassed, now intrigued man was doing the same.

'What's this?' DC Rushton asked, holding a white envelope he had taken from an inside pocket. He carefully opened the envelope, and lifted out a small, tan-coloured scrap about the size of a business card.

'That,' I said, 'is the missing papyrus fragment.'

Chapter Forty-One

'Go on, then,' said Maisy, 'spill the beans. How did you do it?'

I put up a hand, to indicate that Maisy would have to wait. My mouth was still half full of an Italian ciabatta. Molly, Maisy and I had found a table outside Katsouri's, and Molly and I were in the middle of debriefing Maisy about the morning's events.

I swallowed the last crumbs, took a swig of San Pellegrino Limonata, and started replying.

'We hatched it last night,' I said.

'The meeting was already set up with the professor,' said Molly, 'so we didn't think he would suspect anything. Jake is friendly with the staff at Caffè Nero, so they reserved some tables for us.' She resumed eating her bagel with smoked salmon and cream cheese. I took up the story again.

'First of all, we contacted DS Penry. I told her what I thought had happened, and that maybe I could get the professor to talk about it. She was less keen on trying to intercept a handover with Brad Ryan. It could happen anywhere, and she didn't have the budget to tail both of them.'

Maisy nodded. 'That makes sense. If it had been drugs, maybe they'd want both parties. But with an artefact the priority would be to shut down the operation as soon as possible and hope to get the artefact back.'

'We went for belt and braces in recording him,' said Molly. 'I rigged up a radio mike linked to an audio recorder and taped the mike under the table. I picked it up in the morning after I left Jake's.'

Maisy raised an eyebrow. 'You stayed over, cousin?'

I blushed.

Molly laughed. 'Not like that. Someone had to stay with Jake after his head injury. He got the couch, I got his bed.'

'What head injury?' asked Maisy.

'I banged my head badly, so I needed to go to A&E. Molly took me. We ended up with some time to kill while we were waiting, so we did all the planning and phone calls there.'

'And are you okay now?'

'I'm fine,' I said. And mostly I was. Just a slight ache, dulled with paracetamol. I took another bite of ciabatta, enjoying the mix of sweet peppers, tangy cheese and spicy meats.

'How did it happen? Did you fall?'

Molly and I had decided not to tell anyone else, even Maisy, about Craig, Axel and Spud. The fewer people who knew, the better. We didn't want to put Maisy at risk, and we had no intention of ever having anything to do with them again.

'Slipped, fell, hit the back of my head. Boring but painful.'

Maisy brought the conversation back to the events of today.

'How could you be sure that the table you had rigged up would be free, and that none of the others would be?'

'We filled them all up,' I said. 'I phoned up Jemma Williamson, the reporter, and invited her along, so she went nearest the door. She had never met the professor face to face, but had only spoken to him over the phone earlier in the week. Then came the rigged table, and I persuaded my neighbour Mo to come into town and sit there. DI Penry took the next table. That was a bit of a risk; she had met the professor briefly. But she kept her back turned the whole time. And then the next table was Molly.'

Molly took over the story.

'Then we just waited inside the café until Jake and the professor came in. Mo stood up just when they were looking for tables, to make sure that the only free one was the one I'd taped the mike to.'

Maisy shook her head slightly. 'I can't believe it worked. What if he had realised he was being recorded?'

'Then we were no worse off,' I said. 'But he did find out, and weirdly it worked to our advantage. Once he'd turned off the iPhone recorder, it never occurred to him he was still being recorded. He just relaxed, and wanted to show how clever he was.'

'He is such an arrogant man,' Maisy said.

'Arrogant is the word. Can you believe he kept the papyrus fragment in his pocket? The nerve of the man,' I said.

'What an idiot. Wasting his entire career for this. I wonder what it will mean for the project, with him gone?

And when does your suspension officially get lifted?' asked Maisy.

'Well, the trustees will have plenty to discuss when they meet tomorrow. I'm still scheduled to go and speak to them. I suppose they'll lift it then.'

Maisy finished off her ciabatta, and wiped her mouth with a paper napkin. She stood up, saying, 'They've asked to see me too. Anyway, some of us need to get back to work. See you, Jake. See you, cuz.' Maisy walked off down Deansgate towards the dark red of the John Rylands, leaving Molly and me alone again.

I shifted awkwardly in my chair, glancing over at Molly's lively eyes and flowing hair.

'I know we've been thrown together a lot the past couple of days...' I drew to a halt.

Molly took another bite of bagel, finishing it off, and nodded, looking up at me expectantly.

I started feeling my cheeks burning again, and someone was tying up my intestines into different knots.

'I was sort of wondering whether you'd like to go on a proper date. A normal one?'

A sadness crept into Molly's eyes, and she looked at me seriously.

'On our first date, I got kidnapped, threatened with GBH, involved with a drug gang and spent half the evening in hospital. Counting today as our second date, I've spent it covertly recording a criminal professor, providing evidence for the police, and potentially getting my face in the national newspapers, which I do not consider a positive,' she said.

'At least it hasn't been boring,' I said.

'No, no-one can accuse it of being boring. The problem has been in the opposite direction. It has been too interesting.

You know, like that curse, "may you live in interesting times". Well, these have been interesting times.'

'So...' I said, unsure where this was heading, but not liking the journey.

'So I think it's a bit too rich for me. I've only just moved to Manchester, I'm starting a new job next week, and this is too much on top of everything else. I really like you, but I don't think this is a good time to start a new relationship.'

'Oh,' I said. 'Will I still see you again?'

'I'm sure our paths will cross occasionally. You work with my cousin, and so we're bound to bump into each other from time to time.' She got up, took her black bag full of audio equipment off the back of her chair, smiled, and came closer.

She leant over, gave me a gentle kiss on the cheek, smiled, and said, 'Goodbye, Jake. It's been memorable'. Then she walked off down John Dalton Street, hair waving in the breeze, taking her bag and my heart with her.

Chapter Forty-Two

My phone woke me from a deep, dreamless sleep on Friday morning. I groaned, and reached over to see who would think that calling at seven in the morning was appropriate.

'Hello mum,' I said, yawning. 'Why are you phoning so early?'

'Don't be ridiculous. It's not early at all. I've been up for hours. Well, an hour. Anyway, you're in the newspaper again. But they don't say much. Just that "a man has been charged." Is that you?'

I yawned again before replying. 'No, mum, that isn't me. Otherwise, I wouldn't be in bed being woken by you, but in a prison cell somewhere. It was my boss. He got arrested for nicking the papyrus.'

'Well, why don't they say more in the papers? They really didn't say much at all.'

'He got arrested, so the papers can't say much now until after the trial. That's when the full story will come out. If they published anything now, they could be done for contempt of court.'

'Well,' she said, in a sniffy tone, 'it's most unsatisfactory. Anyway, the other day you were on the loo or something, and your friend called on your behalf. He said you were sending a parcel to me. When should I expect to receive it? And is it a surprise? And do you still have the runs?'

I cursed silently. Now I would have to think of a random present to send to my parents unlinked to any occasion.

'It might be a few days. You know what the post is like nowadays.' Blaming the post in Britain has been a national pastime for decades.

'I was speaking to Anne about you yesterday. Do you know how she referred to you? "How is your notorious son?" she said. I hardly knew where to look. Notorious. She made being in the papers sound so... seedy.'

My ploy to emphasise my fame had backfired.

'Well, I'll be back to normal academic work next week. No more papers to worry about. Nothing for Mrs Barswell to turn her nose up at.'

'And she said that Adam's had a promotion. He's been made a junior partner in the firm. When are you going to get a promotion?'

'That's great news about Adam, isn't it, mum?' I said.

There was a pause.

'Of course it's great news. I'm very pleased for Anne. It would just be nice to have some great news to pass on to her. About your job. Or a relationship. We're not getting any younger, and it would be selfish not to give us grandchildren.'

'Adam's not doing that either,' I said.

'Actually, that was the other part of her news. His girl-friend Louise is pregnant, and they've got engaged. Anne will have a wedding and a grandchild. We're delighted. Obviously.'

I was losing badly in my competition with Adam. That it was a competition that I hadn't entered, that I didn't want to enter, and that my chief competitor was probably utterly oblivious about, was irrelevant according to my mother's logic. I decided to quit while I was behind.

'Listen, mum, I've got a busy day, so I need to go now. Need the loo again. Speak to you soon. Love you. Bye.'

This was a lie. I didn't need the loo. But I did want a bit longer in bed. I felt a little sorry for myself. It was Friday, and in one week I had managed to: find and lose the treasure of a lifetime; be investigated by the police; be suspended from work; follow a range of innocent people around Manchester; be beaten up and threatened by thugs; be involved in a sting operation; and be turned down by a woman I liked and who I had hoped liked me.

I put the phone back on the bedside cabinet and tried to get back to sleep.

Chapter Forty-Three

I pulled the collar of my shirt to try to stop it digging in and tightened my tie again. This made the collar dig in again. I sighed and looked down at my shoes. They were black leather oxfords, which had seen better days. The right shoe had picked up some mud on the journey into town. I tried to rub it off on the back of my left trouser leg, then realised that I now had mud both on my shoe and on my charcoal suit trousers.

I shifted on the hard wooden chair and checked my phone again for the time. It was 11:15am. The trustees were overrunning by quarter of an hour. One of the administrators had found a chair for me to sit on outside the meeting room, and I had been sat on it since for an eternity. Well, at least twenty-five minutes.

I looked down, and wondered about what to do with the bright blue plastic bag at my feet. Inside was a full round of stilton, which later on I would have to wrap up and post to my parents. I sniffed, and realised that people wouldn't need to look inside the bag anyway to guess the contents. The sour, pungent aroma was escaping through the packaging.

The door creaked open, and a tall, balding man in an open shirt, blue blazer and beige chinos peered out.

'Doctor Andrews? Can I call you Jake? I'm Miles Hamer, one of the trustees. Call me Miles. Do you want to come in now?'

I got up, and realised that I would have to take the bag in with me. Unattended bags could set off all sorts of security alerts.

'Jake is fine, thanks. Yes.'

I picked up the bag and followed him in.

Two men and one woman were seated either side of a long, mahogany board table. The rich, chestnut colouring contrasted sharply with piles of white paper and documents scattered near each person. With the oak panelled walls, the room emanated a century of wood polish and serious work.

'Please take a seat here,' said Miles, smiling and indicating a wooden chair with a leather seat chair at the end of the table.

I pulled it back to sit in it, surprised by the solid weight of the chair. Even the furniture had a heavy solemnity. Once I had sat down, I placed the blue bag under the chair.

'Let's do the introductions,' said Miles. 'Everybody, this is Doctor Jake Andrews, one of our postdocs currently working on the James Grove Collection. But I think you probably already know that, especially if you read the papers.'

Everyone chuckled. I tried to smile.

'Jake, just so we're clear we are the projects subcommittee of the full trustee board of the Friends of John Rylands, and we are the funders of your project. Closest to you on your left is Amanda.' Amanda looked to be about fifty.

Her hair was long and loose, light brown with grey streaks. She wore thin, gold-rimmed glasses and a long floral-patterned dress. She smiled at me as her name was mentioned.

'And opposite Amanda closest to you is Nawshad.' He had friendly eyes, dark hair, glasses, and was in a dark green polo shirt and denim jeans.

Nawshad smiled, and said, 'I hope you didn't dress smartly on our account. We're pretty informal here.'

'No, no problem at all,' I said. It had been the first time I had worn the suit since a family wedding the previous summer. I was hot, uncomfortable and itching.

'And last but not least, next to Nawshad is Anthony.' Anthony was also in a suit, navy in his case. A bright red tie proudly drew attention against a crisp white shirt. I noticed he was sporting gold cufflinks that looked old. Anthony nodded, but didn't smile.

Miles sat down next to Amanda, and scrolled with a mouse on his open laptop.

'Here we go. Agenda item 78. The James Grove Collection Project update. Well, this last week has been very exciting, hasn't it?' He looked up from the screen and smiled at me again.

'You could say that', I replied.

'Things got a bit sticky for you at the start of the week, we believe, but there's a bit more clarity now. Obviously, the professor has been suspended pending the results of the criminal investigation. For the time being it's just you and Maisy running the project.'

'Does that mean that you've formally revoked my suspension?' I asked.

All of the trustees looked puzzled.

'We don't do that,' Miles said. 'Technically, you're employed by the University of Manchester, as the Library is part of the University. We control some funding, but we can't make that type of personnel decision. We'd need to get HR involved. And we simply haven't had time since Monday to sort that.'

'When will they be able to revoke the suspension?' I asked.

'There's nothing to revoke,' said Miles.

'Wait,' I said, cogs turning in my brain, 'so I was never officially suspended? Professor Chelworth told me I was.'

'Well, he had no right to do that.' Miles seemed more offended by the professor breaking proper protocol than by forgery and fraud.

'Anyway, we were going to address a recommendation for possible suspension in this meeting, but events have overtaken that issue, so we didn't need to involve the University. We've got a couple of pieces of news that affect the project.' He searched through a few documents on the desk, each a few pages thick stapled together.

'Here we go. First, with Professor Chelworth suspended – the University did that themselves as soon as he'd been charged; we just got informed afterwards – the project needs someone to head it up.'

My ears pricked up at this. Could this be the promotion my mother had been hoping for? And a promotion might also mean a pay increase, which would be welcome. Maybe I could even afford to run a car, although insurance in my part of Manchester was hideously expensive. And having a promotion would also make it easier to apply for a tenured post when this project ended.

'You'll be pleased to know we've decided to appoint your

colleague Doctor Maisy Roberts as acting head of the project. We know you both get on, and after the... excitement of the last week, we thought having her calm head would help get things back on track. Make sure the donors are happy.'

Inside, my brief daydreams of success came crashing down like a house of cards caught in a breeze. My mother's hopes, my car and my career would have to wait.

'That's fantastic news,' I said, 'she'll be excellent in the role. It's well deserved.'

And I wasn't even lying. Maisy was a superb scholar and reliable in all areas. If I was being honest, she would definitely do a better job at running the project than I would have.

At this point Amanda took over from Miles.

'And we've got some other news, hot off the press,' she said. 'The events of this last week haven't been great publicity for the project, so we're looking for some good PR.'

I nodded in what I hoped was an intelligent manner.

'Anyway,' she continued, 'a local school are holding an exhibition of a papyrus fragment as part of a summer open day.'

'That sounds very... worthy,' I said, trying to see where this was going.

'And it's not just any old fragment, it's from the Gospel of Thomas.'

My eyes opened wider. 'How did a school get hold of something like that?' I asked. But even as I asked, I realised what the answer probably was.

'When Grenfell and Hunt came back with their finds from Oxyrhynchus, some of the papyri were donated to schools.'

I repeated my intelligent nodding look, and tried to show

that I did know what I was talking about. Oxyrhynchus was the site in Egypt that housed a large rubbish dump excavated by Grenfell and Hunt, Oxford professors, around the beginning of the twentieth century. The dump had contained a treasure trove of ancient papyri, with some containing the earliest known texts of plays, poems and religious texts.

'Yes, they distributed some of the papyri beyond Oxford,' I said. 'We've got some here in Manchester, both with us and with the Manchester Museum. But I thought the only schools that they donated to were the posh ones in the south. Eton, Charterhouse, Westminster, that type of place.'

Nawshad took over from Amanda.

'It turns out that one of Hunt's best friends was an old boy of a school here in South Manchester, and they ended up with this Thomas fragment. It's Greek, second to third century.'

'And what do they want us to do?' I asked.

'They'd like an expert to help them with a little exhibition, with the unveiling of the Thomas fragment being the opening event. It's been hidden away most of the time since they got it. But now it's around one hundred years since the original donation, so that's the push for why now.'

'And they want our help?' I said.

Nawshad shook his head.

'They don't want our help,' he said, 'they want your help. You in particular. And in return they're willing to make a most generous donation to the Friends of John Rylands.'

I blinked a couple of times. This made little sense.

'Me? Me, in particular? Why do they want me?'

As I was saying this, I realised perhaps I should not have seemed so astonished in front of the trustees. Fortunately, none of them seemed to notice.

'Funny story. One of the sixth form, a girl, has been pushing the project in the school. Loves history, that type of thing. Anyway, her father is a big donor to the school, and is covering all the costs of the exhibition, including insurance.'

'Yes...' I said cautiously, unclear as to how this involved me.

Nawshad smiled at me, and said, 'Well, apparently the father knows you. Anyway, he contacted us yesterday suggesting that you are seconded to the school for the duration of the exhibition, to work with the school's history department and his daughter and some other sixth formers.'

I began to put the puzzle together. An ominous connection was forming in my mind.

'Would the father be called, by any chance, Mister Craig Bloodsmith, and the daughter Megan?'

Nawshad beamed. 'You do know him. Excellent. He said something about it being great to work with you. He said he hoped you weren't too tied up in other things.'

I tried not to let the inward groan show on my face. I had hoped never again to cross paths with Craig Bloodsmith.

Nawshad continued, 'That's happening in just a few weeks, so it's likely to take up most of your time. It's the Manchester Millworkers School. Set up in Victorian times for the orphans and widows of millworkers. Private now, of course. The school want to do a big publicity blitz around this exhibition, tie it in with their motto: "Weaving the future together".'

Miles came back in. 'And we want our share of that publicity blitz. The more goodwill we can generate, the better.'

I considered the situation. It would be unlikely that Craig would be in school for much of the time; his gang-related activities would presumably need tending to. And putting on an exhibition would look good on my CV when applying for tenure. Plus, it was a chance to work closely with a significant papyrus. Perhaps things were looking up.

'One more thing, Jake,' said Miles. 'Your main contact with the school will be from their external relations department. Apparently, someone new, doing a mat-leave cover. You'll be working closely with...' he looked down and checked his notes, 'a woman called Molly Leyser. Will that be okay?'

That would definitely be okay.

The End

Author's Notes

The genesis for this book was a tweet (in the days when Twitter was the official name). Dr Andrew Jacobs, who researches the interplay between the cultural place of the Bible in society and the fiction genre of gospel thrillers, reposted a picture of a gospel thriller generator, created by Colin Whiting. You matched up the first letter of your first name with part of the title, and similarly with the first letter of the surname. With J and T I was presented with 'The Magdalene Secret' as my gospel thriller. And that's when I decided to write the book of the title. So my first thanks go to Colin Whiting, and Andrew Jacobs. At the time of writing you can find a copy at https://scalar.usc.edu/works/gospel-thrillers/extras-reviews-interviews-and-other-media.2.

The hero's name, Jacob Andrews, is a little homage to the real doctor, but my hero is otherwise completely fictional, as are all the characters in the book. Any resemblance to real people is purely coincidental. (And if my mother ever reads this bit, you are utterly unlike Jake's mum, thank goodness).

The places in the book are often real. The John Rylands

University Library is a genuine Manchester institution: a world-leading repository of papyri and books housed in a neo-gothic building worth visiting in its own right. Many years ago, I worked in the library on my PhD thesis, and I encourage anyone visiting Manchester to drop in. It's a fantastic place with fantastic people.

Katsouri's and Caffè Nero are also real places on Deansgate in Manchester, and the Midland hotel has been one of the top hotels in the city for over a century. The Waterstone's on Deansgate is the city's biggest bookshop, a great place to browse (there's a café on one of the floors). Manchester Cathedral is another worthwhile site to visit. If you have children, see if they can discover all the bees (the symbol of Manchester) scattered throughout (hint: look on the back of chairs; stained glass windows; and even the roof).

The Magdalene Initiative is not real, and neither is the Prince Edward Hotel. Also invented is the police station to which Jake gets taken.

Fallowfield, where Jake lives, is a lively mix of students and locals. The Greek place near Sainsbury's mentioned in the book is Tzatziki's, and I recommend it.

The papyri collection mentioned in the book is fictional, but Grenfell and Hunt, the pioneers of papyri collecting, did bring back boxes that they had bought alongside finds excavated from various Egyptian locations.

Papyri forgeries are ubiquitous. Good ones can take years to detect as being fakes, and can initially fool even worldwide experts. The techniques named in the book to authenticate finds, such as carbon dating, raman spectroscopy and palaeography, are some of a wide range of considerations.

Scandals involving papyri are also not uncommon. The Museum of the Bible paid about $7 million for papyri, only to later discover that they had been sold illegitimately, belonging to the Egypt Exploration Society (an organisation dating back to Victorian times that has a long association with papyri finds). The Museum returned the papyri.

The hero's experience of being on a short-term contract despite being an experienced post-doctoral researcher is typical, part of a current crisis in the humanities.

I was first introduced to the study of papyri by Dr Roberta Mazza (an expert both on papyri and the illegal trade surrounding them). She introduced me to Bagnall, Papyri.info and the murky world of selling papyri, both genuine and forgeries (check out her book *Stolen Fragments*). Any mistakes in the book are despite, not because, of what I learned from her. The name Maisy Roberts is another little homage.

There are countless people who have helped along the way, including Dr Janet Lees, who read an initial draft, my wonderful colleagues at the Luther King Centre for Theology and Ministry, my friends and family. My thanks to all of you.

Printed in Great Britain
by Amazon